KNOCKING ON HELEN'S DOOR

NEW YORK TIMES BESTSELLING AUTHOR

EVE LANGLAIS

PROLOGUE

THE NINTH RING WAS GONE. It didn't matter how many times Lucifer replayed its end, it remained missing.

Lucifer's office wall flickered as images played upon it, Hell's version of surveillance. The fine-tuned magic paused videos and tagged them if the esoteric algorithms detected items of interest. Underlings usually handled the monitoring of juicy bits, but for certain items, the devil himself needed to take a closer look.

Lucifer stood in front of the many scrolling images, his gaze unfocused, his mind empty. In this state of relaxation, it proved easy to zoom in on footage of interest. By simply willing it, the entire wall became an aerial view of the eighth ring, skinnier than before, having lost a few feet. Overtaken by the Wilds.

Or so he assumed. Could also be the ring had shrunk. Lucifer hated to admit he didn't quite understand what was happening. If he were asked to guess, he'd say the Wilds beyond his kingdom was expanding, moving the border of its domain to overtake Hell.

And not just take but remake. The ninth ring used to have towns, not the most elaborate setup, yet there were buildings and roads. Not anymore. They'd vanished and didn't leave behind any rubble. The Wilds took and reshaped in its image. Without warning. Not even a scream.

Whole hamlets disappeared when it first started. Citizens—the damned and demonic alike—went to bed and were never seen again.

Which led to other villages grabbing their shit and fleeing. At least the smart ones did. No one knew what happened to those who were absorbed by the Wilds. No one wanted to find out.

The refugees from the ninth ring crowded the eighth and seventh. His aerial eye in the sky dipped and zipped in and out of buildings, taking stock of the situation. Overcrowded, and the mood highly anxious, which led to greater than usual violence. A powder keg ready to explode. He'd need to act before things got too critical.

The towns in the eighth ring overflowed with citizens, the noise and uncertainty a troubling hum that permeated the air. The amount of people crammed in there disquieted, but the fact the eighth ring didn't bulge as fatly as the day before gave him a more intense chill than the time Hell froze over.

Apparently, it wasn't enough that he lost people to the growing Wilds. He now also had citizens fleeing into it. He'd even caught groups of them on surveillance, entire families with no possessions in hand or on their backs, walking into the Wilds and not coming back, which wasn't entirely surprising. The Wilds didn't treat visitors kindly, yet the idiots kept wandering in there.

Why did they do it? Did they hear or sense something in there? Because he sure as fuck didn't.

The video lifted from the eighth ring and focused on where the Wilds spread. Stunted and twisted trees, boggy swamps, even grassy fields with blades sharp as daggers. A veritable jungle that turned gray as he watched, a mist seeping up over the highest treetops, spreading over fields. Obscuring all.

Fascinating. He snapped his fingers, and an imp appeared. "I'm going to send you to the border. I want you to take three steps into the fog then return immediately and report."

"Yes, Dark Lord."

Lucifer snapped his fingers again and watched on screen as his imp appeared and immediately leaped into the fog.

Didn't return.

So he sent another.

And another.

By the sixty-ninth, his daughter Bambi appeared. "I hear you're decimating your army."

He glared. "There's something wrong with the Wilds." A problem with the fog at the very least. No one had returned. Every single person who went in stayed in. Even those with instructions to turn right back around.

It didn't help the fog mocked by taking another foot off the eighth ring.

What the fuck was going on? Did the Wilds—an ungoverned, unmapped place beyond the nine rings of Hell—still exist under the gray mist? Was it the Wilds or something else eating his kingdom?

"You're right. I'm wasting my time sending minions. I need hunters. Good ones who won't die within the first step or get distracted if there happens to be buxom nymphs on the other side." Lucifer owned the souls of many who'd gotten killed because they stared at boobs.

"You know of a hunter that won't be distracted by nymphs?" Bambi asked, putting a hand on her hip, drawing attention to her business suit, snug in all the right places but not revealing any cleavage or thigh.

It brought a frown to the devil's face. "Are you okay? You've been dressing awfully conservatively lately."

"Sometimes less is more. Which you should know. You haven't worn any of your capes in a while."

Because every time he did, someone threw up on it. He'd tried wearing it by himself, hiding in his closet, drinking to the good ol' days, and ended up puking on it.

"My cape days are over. Long live the fanny pack." Better than a diaper bag. He kept everything he needed in it, including a fake identity and cash to start over somewhere in South America.

"Fanny packs are a thing of the past. It's now the era of the crossbody satchel."

"Satchels are back?" His expression brightened. "Do you know how much you can fit in those?" He might be able to sneak in a dragon because even the Dark Lord never knew when he'd need a dragon.

"Might be a good idea for everyone to start carrying one given what's going on." Bambi pointed to the screen. "This is not good."

"I know. Which is why I'll send Teivel in for a peek." One of Lucifer's finest hunters. A vampire who'd served him many years until his daughter stole him for her harem.

Bambi cackled. "You're kidding, right? Muriel will lose her shit if you ask."

Muriel being one of his daughters. Disrespectful as fuck, which really made him proud and angry all at once.

"Why would she say no? It's for the good of the kingdom."

"Go ahead and call her. Ask. See how that goes." Bambi offered him a smirk he'd perfected over the centuries.

"I will call her. She'll understand the seriousness of the situation and totally agree we have to send our best to fix it." He rang his daughter, his latest Helldroid phone crackling in his ear. Electronics, even infused with magic, didn't fare well on the Hell plane.

Muriel replied after two rings, sounding out of breath. "Daddy, dearest, your timing is shitty as always."

"Once a cock blocker, always a cock blocker."

That drew a giggle from Muriel. "Who says she's got a cock?"

His brows rose. "You took another?"

5

"Thinking about it. Problem being, then I'd have to share her with my boys. I kind of like being the only woman in the mix." She gasped and laughed then obviously spoke to someone else as she said, "Brat. I'll get you back for that."

"This is actually great news. Since you don't currently have need of Teivel's dick, can I borrow him for a teensy tiny job?"

"What job?" Muriel's humor immediately faded.

"I just need him to check out the Wilds. Make sure things are okay."

"Like fuck." Low and firm. "I heard what happened to the minor demons you sent in."

News got around much too quickly when it was bad. "Obviously, their minds weren't strong enough to fight whatever allure lies within."

"Teivel isn't going."

Pride and annoyance warred within him at her firmness and refusal to obey. "He's the best hunter I've got."

"Still a no. We've all seen what happens in the movies when people walk into mysterious fogs and mists," Muriel reminded.

"Good point." It was why, despite his curiosity, Lucifer hadn't yet gone himself. First rule of laziness, delegate! "Well, then, I guess I should let you return to your debauchery."

"Your jealousy is showing."

Was it? Probably. He'd had some epic orgies in his time. Damn Gaia for insisting on monogamy. "Have fun with your new partner."

"I will." With a giggle, his daughter hung up and he sighed.

Bambi eyed him. "Let me guess, she said no."

"Utterly disrespectful and disobedient. Just for that, I'm going to throttle her internet again."

"Way to act your age."

"If I acted my age, I would have her decapitated," he growled. "I need to do something about that fog." Which was why he next sent in some prisoners with one instruction: go in and return for forgiveness of their sins.

They disappeared the moment they stepped past the border of what had been the ninth ring. For all he knew they turned to dust or mooned him. He never found out. The fog hid all.

And obsessed him even after Bambi left claiming she had a date. With who? A Mormon? Because she was wearing way too many clothes.

A mere thought opened a portal. He stepped through and stood in front of the swirling mist. Not having bothered to change, he wore his slippers—the bunny ones with floppy ears, red eyes, and fangs—along with a robe, the rich burgundy of it trimmed in gold thread.

He eyed the fog. Dense enough to foil sight.

He sniffed. No scent.

He held out a hand and stuck it inside. He couldn't see it at all. He let it sit there for a few seconds before pulling it back to see if it had disintegrated. The flesh didn't slough, nor did he sense any moisture.

Strange.

Perhaps a giant fan would blow the mist away?

If only it were that simple.

For a brief moment, he thought about putting his face in the fog and taking a deep breath. Could be the fog emitted a drug that enticed his citizens into entering.

He stepped close enough the toes of his sleepers disappeared past the edge. He just had to lean forward.

Lucifer stepped back. He didn't have time to enjoy a good hallucination. Fate of Hell and all that. Not mention, he had to be careful. Drugs often had the side effect of making him hornier than usual and led to some epic sexcapades. While he wouldn't mind some good harem action, his wife would bitch. Spoilsport.

His study of the fog was interrupted by the strident voice of a damned soul. "Alonzo, don't go in there," a woman pleaded. "Please."

The man, the big burly sort, who, in a previous life, probably had the nickname Tiny, smiled at the woman —who'd managed to find enough plaid fabric in Hell to make a shirt. Alonzo had a vacuous expression. "Can't you hear them calling?"

"Hear who?" asked the woman, looking perplexed.

Lucifer was wondering the same damned thing. He cocked an ear but only heard a sob as Alonzo tore free from the woman's grip and disappeared from sight, into the mist.

A moment later, a group of hellcats charged past the woman's shaking body. Five of them, eyes rolling and wild as they barreled into the fog.

Oh fuck no. He couldn't afford to lose any more

minions. His legions were already winnowed as it were from recent skirmishes and low birth rates.

He shouldn't panic yet. In the past, Lucifer had enjoyed lesser numbers than this—especially after that hundred-year war with his brother. If he'd only had a few more dragons, he wouldn't have had to agree to the pesky clause in their treaty that restricted him from openly interfering on Earth.

So, he did it subtly, and when his minions got caught, he pled innocent. In other words, lied.

But he couldn't keep hiding the calamity befalling his kingdom. The Wilds and this fog were only the newest threat. He also dealt with a diminishing number of souls and a drastically lower demonic birth rate. Which reminded him, Grim Dating appeared to be having success on Earth.

Now if only Heaven would stop meddling.

1

HELEN STOOD alongside Michelina in the gestational receiving area—a fancy name for a rooftop where they awaited a pair of incoming storks—trying not to collapse out of boredom. Notice had been received to expect two deliveries, but they weren't given an exact time. It necessitated them getting in place just after dawn.

From their spot, Helen could see the entire nursery quadrangle. Rather than walls to protect the cherubs within, they'd erected a massive windowless building several stories in height, shaped as a hollow circle with only an arch leading out. The gestational receiving tower that they stood on squatted in comparison, jutting from the middle of a park bisected by winding stone paths.

Helen rocked on her heels, restlessness making her fidget. The noon hour had come and gone without seeing a single bird.

"Would you stop jerking around?" Michelina

snapped from where she prayed on her knees. She had her head down and hands clasped. She had no problem dropping into a deep prayer for hours on end, whereas Helen had been having issues with patience of late and didn't know why.

She found herself bored. A word that was blasphemy. Boredom didn't exist, just idle hands. She tried keeping busy. Had washed her robe for the next day. Cleaned her room. Not that it ever got dirty. She'd enjoyed the perfect sun with others, sitting on fragrant grass, doing nothing because she'd already read the seven accepted versions of the Bible so many times she knew them by heart.

On days when she didn't have to monitor receiving, she worked in the nursery itself, which she did mostly enjoy. Babies tended to be unpredictable. Helen worked as one of the early caretakers, handling the very youngest with their stunted wings and incomprehensible babble. She changed their diapers and fed them, made sure they got their allocated stimulation time and exercise. During their infant stage, they were malleable, their grace and perfection still to be created. The lessons started young, and by the time they'd reached their adult size, they were ready to receive their task from God and join the other angels.

New batches arrived sporadically, delivered by stork, with the children ranging from very small and useless to able to sit up and babble. She wondered where they came from.

"Where does what come from?" asked Michelina, moving from her knees to stand beside her, patient and serene. Her robes always perfect, her hair blonde and falling in a shiny, straight curtain. Unlike Helen whose curly black hair refused to be tamed, and she always managed to spill something on the front of herself.

"Babies. Where do they come from?" Helen asked.

"The storks," Michelina replied as if it were a matter of fact and in a sense it was. Except...

"But where do the storks find them?" She eyed the perfectly blue sky. She'd never seen it any other way. Never seen anything outside the nursery actually. She'd been raised and then assigned a duty within it.

"I don't know where they find them. Why does it matter?"

Wasn't Michelina curious at all? "I heard someone say they grow in cabbage patches."

An incredulous gaze turned on Helen. "Cherubs are not grown in the dirt."

"Then how? Trees? Eggs?"

"Why does it matter?" Michelina crinkled her nose. "The Lord makes us new brothers and sisters then gives them to the storks to deliver."

The answer didn't satisfy Helen. "How can the Lord be making them? Isn't our Father, who art in heaven, currently being detained?"

Formerly known as God, some said his insistence on being called Elyon was a sign of his madness and why he had been placed inside a secret and secured location by his son, Jesus Christ—who preferred to go by Charlie. He'd said his dad had served the world long and well, and now just needed to rest.

However, if Helen listened to rumors—which she

never ever did because everyone knew they were spread by evil minions—their Lord had not only suffered a mental break, he'd tried to start a war with his brother.

Obviously, that was a lie since their Father was a pacifist. The same couldn't be sure about his son. Charlie was in charge, and things had been changing. Which led her to question if they were all God's children, why was Charlie the chosen heir? There were angels older than him. Why didn't they handle things while Elyon recovered?

"Just because our Father, who gazes upon us in heaven, is currently enjoying a retreat, doesn't mean he's not taking care of us. I also don't understand your obsession. What does it matter where the cherubs come from?"

"Aren't you curious about how babies are made?"

"No."

Helen, however, didn't feel the same. "Remember Loreanna?"

"The one who tried to jump off the building and forgot to fly?" Some said Loreanna tried to commit the sin of suicide.

"Yes. Her. She was taken to a healer for repair, and when she returned"—Helen's voice dropped as she whispered the next juicy tidbit—"she told me humans make babies via a ritual called fornication, where two individuals, a male and female, slot their opposing genital pieces together and create an infant."

Michelina's eyes widened as she exclaimed, "How dare you repeat such filthy gossip. I am going to report you to Archnanny Rafaella." The head angel in charge of all things nursery related. Someone had to manage the cherubs and their caretakers.

"Don't do that." The last time Helen dared to question she spent five hundred days in quiet contemplation in the room of nothing. Meaning she was put in a space with no light, sound, or sensation. She hadn't felt like herself since, and it hadn't cured her desire to know things. And not just where babies came from, but why they couldn't leave the nursery, or better yet, why couldn't she see what lay outside of Heaven? She knew there was a world out there, a dangerous one called Earth. Only the soldiers with the deadly task of defending their realm from the forces of evil—aka Lucifer's legions—could leave Heaven, along with those specially chosen for Guardian Angel duty. Every other angel stayed in their section. Did their job. Lived a perfect life under the eye of their Father—who was being detained in Heaven.

In the last decade, though, she couldn't help but notice the boredom. The stagnancy. The lack of risk of any kind.

They weren't allowed to run, because they might trip.

Laughter, especially the loud kind, was forbidden, as it might interfere with those in quiet contemplation.

No nudity so that no one could feel as if another person's flesh was better than theirs.

The only books allowed were those approved by the Archangels who ran things. Seven books. Only seven and yet she remembered Loreanna telling her that, on Earth, there were millions of stories.

Millions. It sounded impossible. It had to be a lie, but how to know for sure? Helen couldn't ask, or she'd be sent to the quiet place.

She also couldn't scream. Screaming was frowned upon.

No going past the walls of the nursery. No standing on them to gaze longingly at the outside either. The funny part being there was nothing technically stopping her from going, just the rule that said she mustn't.

The list of things they couldn't do filled a scroll several feet long. Some which she didn't understand, like no skateboards. What was a skateboard?

She had no one to answer her questions. As a nursery worker, she was kept to an even stricter set of rules than other angels, or so she was made to understand. As the shaper of young angelic minds, nannies had to remain the purest. The austerity supposedly made them God's favorites.

But if she was favored, how come she'd never even met him? In the Bible, Fathers cared for their children.

A speck in the perfect sky, blue without end, grew into a massive bird, its wings longer than her arms. It banked, and its cargo tilted, the bundled fabric clutched in its talons shifted. A pudgy arm waved free.

And then a body tumbled out.

2

BEFORE MICHELINA UTTERED her shocked gasp, Helen was running for the edge of the tower's roof. She threw herself off, arms outstretched, her wings snapping behind her, halting her plunge, so she could glide and catch the falling baby.

"Hello, little one." Helen smiled, holding the solid frame. The child, wide eyed and startled, held in its yell and beamed back.

Helen landed on the rooftop, and the baby was snatched by Michelina. With lips pursed, she offered a disapproving, "This one will be trouble."

"Because it fell? How is that the child's fault?" Seemed like an accident to her.

"Clearly displaying a rebellious nature. I'll handle its processing while you wait for the next one." Off marched Michelina, body stiff, her long white robes flaring with each snapped step. She showed no comfort to the baby who'd begun to wail. It hurt Helen's heart to hear the child crying. She would have snuggled it close, murmured soft reassurance. However, Michelina wasn't the soft or coddling type of nanny.

With a sigh—because she could hardly criticize the older more experienced angel—she turned to watch the big blue sky. Always the same shade. Never marred or obscured by anything. The bibles spoke of things called clouds and storms. She couldn't fathom what that meant. How frightening it must be to have the sun hidden or for water to fall from the sky. And strong gusts of wind? How would they fly?

The day passed, and the sun set at exactly the same time every day, and her stomach, trained to know what it meant, grumbled in hunger. Dinnertime and no second baby. Rather than leave immediately, she stood and watched the unfolding canvas of color, spectacular and vivid. The exact same medley of colors that she'd seen the last time she was outdoors for a sunset, and the time before, and the time before that. It never, ever changed.

Sunrise would occur with the same precision. Not that she'd see it in her windowless room. She was usually eating breakfast, although, in her younger years, she'd skipped that first meal to be outside and watch it. The novelty wore off quickly, especially since missing breakfast left her with nothing until dinner.

Her lessons claimed that on Earth—past the pearly gates into a mist that no one but their brave soldiers dared enter—no sunrise or sunset was ever the same. Her teachers taught that Earth was a place of chaos and evil. Of sin and damnation. Where humans strived to recreate Heaven and failed miserably.

And she'd believed in that until, during one of their stork watches, Betty recited a rumor she'd heard. A rumor that humans were God's children. Blasphemy, of course. Angels were nothing like those hairy, smelly beasts. Not that she'd ever met one, but by their description in the Bible, they were primitive.

When Loreanna returned, she told the same story as Betty had, with more details. She claimed they were being lied to. That humans and Earth were wonderful compared to Heaven. And then one day she was gone. The Archnanny never explained where she went. Loreanna never came back.

Nobody who left the nursery ever returned, not even the babies Helen helped care for. Once they reached a certain age, unless they were assigned to be nannies, they departed and never returned.

Helen often wondered what her life would be like outside the nursery. Wished she could have been posted as a guard, as they appeared to have more freedom to roam.

The sun set. With twilight making it hard to see, and still no stork, she couldn't wait any longer. She would have to let the Archnanny know. All angels were to be inside before twilight ended and night began.

"Why can't we go outside at night?" she'd innocently asked.

"Because bad things happen at night," her teacher told her.

"What kind of bad things?"

The teacher, who didn't like being questioned, gave Helen a hundred days in solitary, a sealed room with only what she needed to contemplate her faith until she agreed Heaven and its rules protected her. Her Father, who ruled Heaven, hallowed be his name, only wanted to keep her safe. How could she be so ungrateful?

She went inside before dusk ended and never rose before the sun tickled the sky. She couldn't help but recall Betty, who'd giggled when asked where she got her information about humans and earth. She claimed to go out at night and to be in love with one of Heaven's soldiers. Carnal love.

Which was forbidden!

Probably why Betty eventually disappeared.

If Helen wasn't careful, she'd end up punished, too. Never question. Her Father, who made rules in Heaven, knew best.

She headed down from the rooftop and fetched her dinner. A bowl of gruel, filling and satisfying. The flavor and texture were the same for every meal. It never changed, just like her evening routine remained consistent. Wash her dishes. Say her prayers. Then go to bed.

Except for the umpteenth night in a row, Helen found herself too restless to sleep. She rose from her pallet and paced her room, three strides by three strides. All the room she needed for a bed, a chair, and a desk. It was greed to want more space. What should have been satisfying felt confining. She tugged at her night robe, snug to the neck and billowy to make her shapeless. Her wings were tucked away for easier sleeping on the bed. She'd not yet reached the age where she preferred to roost.

One, two, three, pivot. One two, three. Flip. It agitated her she couldn't move farther. There was a park outside where she usually walked a good portion of the day. Roof duty meant she'd not gotten enough exercise. If she could just walk off the restless energy surely she would sleep?

She couldn't leave. One of their rules, strictly enforced, was curfew. No angels out after dark.

She eyed her door. What would happen if she went for a walk? Unlike Betty, she wouldn't sin with any soldiers but pray as she went for a stroll within the nursery courtyard.

Two circuits and then back to bed. Before she knew it, she stood outside her room.

The hallway, lined with doors identical to hers, remained empty and quiet. She hustled to the far end and the stairs, expecting to hear a shout.

She went around and around down the stairs to the main level and paused as she finally heard sound. A rustle of fabric then voices. She hugged the wall, her chest thumping as she worried about getting caught.

"Hey, Andreas," a lilting voice said.

Helen frowned as she tried to place it.

A deeper tone replied, "I brought you a present."

"Really? Let's go to my room and you can show me."

Helen heard the rustle as they moved and the snick of a door shutting. Only after thirty breaths of silence did she ease out of the stairwell, the door soundlessly swinging shut after her.

She tiptoed quickly to the door leading outside, only to pause at the threshold. Once she stepped outside, she'd be in trouble. Right now, if caught, she could claim she'd woken and thought it was past dawn. No windows meant no light. She'd claim her internal clock must be off.

She'd lie.

Her eyes widened. How far was she willing to go to break the rules?

Shoving open the door, she put a toe on the tile past the ledge. It didn't get zapped. No alarm went off. Next, she eased her whole body outside. Waited for someone to question her wandering.

Nothing moved. Nor did she perceive any noise. She glanced around to find a different Heaven than she knew during the day.

For one, no blue skies, but so many stars casting a silvery glow. How pretty. She didn't see the fabled moon and wondered if it even shone in Heaven.

The starlight proved enough to outline in stark relief the jutting monolith of a building that housed the rooms for the nursery and teaching staff and the wards for the babies. Three levels circling around the park. Windowless. And even if it weren't, who would see her? Everyone was supposed to be asleep. From the voices she'd heard during her escape outside, she already knew not everyone was, but that worked to her advantage. The guardian angel that protected from the rooftop was in a nanny's bedroom. Doing what?

None of her business. With him gone, this was her chance.

She took a few more steps, enough for the door to close behind her. *Click.*

Hopefully not locked. From sunrise to sunset, the door was open.

The flutter in her stomach wasn't entirely fear but excitement. She moved from her dorm to the park that lay at the center of the courtyard, pleased to see the paths lit by glowing orbs set in stakes.

It was lovely; however, it did make her wonder about the curfew at night. Why have the place lit if not for use? In the daytime, it was a busy place for the nannies to take the cherubs out for a stroll. Yet as she strode along the straight paths that bisected the park with its perfectly shaped bushes, she saw no one else. Was she the only one to ever dare walk outside at night?

I'm such a rebel. It made her giddy.

And bold.

If everyone was inside, there was no one to see. Helen flew to the top of the building and froze, waiting for an outcry. When none came, she glanced around for the first time. She saw more monoliths, massive contained areas. Were they also nurseries or the homes of the soldiers and the others who left?

The sudden flicker of starlight drew her gaze, and she noticed a shadow flying overhead. Someone else was out there. She almost dropped back into the nursery garden.

Almost. Instead, emboldened, she took flight, feeling exposed and hidden all at once. Exhilaration filled her as she coasted cool air currents and soared over places like the nursery, if differing in size. Some with illuminated courtyards, others dark and barren.

Past the group of twelve buildings, she found herself coasting over a vast expanse of fog. It covered the ground and scared her, pimpling her skin.

She'd not ever flown so far before. Usually only short trips around the courtyard, teaching the little angels to fly.

It was more enjoyable than expected.

She angled and pumped her wings to get higher, her view expanding, and she gasped. For ahead she saw lights. Lots of bright lights, small squat buildings with roads between them, and no high walls.

3

HELEN NEARED the edge of the lit area. Feeling exposed, she dropped to skim over the fog before immersing herself in it. It dampened the skin but didn't appear to sodden her robe. Her feet hit the ground, and she stumbled for a second before catching herself.

She walked in the direction of the lights, the mist fading as she reached a row of stakes planted in a line that kept the fog from drifting farther.

Hands clasped tight in nervousness, she stepped into the light. No one yelled, but to her surprise, she heard voices. She moved to the nearest building, a single-floor structure with a wide window and a door.

It was dark, but the next window cast a glow. She crept close for a peek and blinked at the sight. Angels, their wings ghostly gossamer at their backs, sat in a group, conversing, not praying. Fraternizing! Rule breakers like her.

She thought about knocking, only to hesitate. What if they turned her in? She had to know more.

Helen traversed past that building and found herself in a maze of hundreds. Only a small portion bore illumination, enough to move swiftly, as she wondered if this place was even part of Heaven. It resembled nothing she'd ever imagined. For one, not everyone was asleep like at the nursery. A male angel wearing a tunic and pants suddenly opened a door.

He stared at her then smiled. "Hello there. Want to come in?" He winked and stood aside.

Rather than reply, she ran. Impulse made her weave in and out of streets until she was utterly lost.

Hugging herself, she began to regret having broken the rules. She just wanted to go home. She glanced up and wondered if she could climb to a rooftop. There wasn't space enough to launch from here.

Once more, a door opened, and rather than wait for them to ask questions, she slid into a dark alley. She crossed it, only to find herself pausing. From a dimly outlined door— light creeping past its edges—she could hear a rhythmic beat, as if someone played music but in a way she'd never imagined. It didn't resemble at all the Heavenly choir they got to listen to during their weekly mass.

For a moment, she moved closer, intrigued and, at the same time, disturbed by the strong, thumping beat. She placed her hand on the door and felt it vibrate under her fingers.

What did they listen to? Could this be the devil music she'd learned about in school? They'd brushed over it in theology, and she'd often wondered what exactly it sounded like.

It was exhilarating, and she found herself moving in time to it, her hips twitching. Her body undulated in a sinuous way that was surely a sin.

Shocked, and a little worried, she moved away from the music—ran actually—until she spilled onto another road. More angels strolled along laughing, sinning by all appearances.

Helen kept jogging, past buildings that were eventually spaced out enough she could fly, but by now she could see a park up ahead with tall trees offering cover. The moment she stepped within, she realized others shared it with her. She heard soft murmurs and husky laughter. A rare noise usually uttered by the cherubs and quickly shushed. Mature angels did not guffaw.

She'd never understood. How could laughter be a sin?

The pure pleasure of it drew her along the spiral path between the twining garden of trees, each the exact same width, height, and number of leaves. That forest gave way to metal shapes. Gray-, gold-, and silver-hued, their forms were indistinct in the wispy clouds clinging to them. They were spread out around a tall hedge that showed a path leading into it.

She didn't plan to go in, but voices from behind spurred her. She entered and peeked to see a pair of soldiers emerge from the tree line, and head for the hedges!

Not wanting to get caught, she sped down the path, looking for another exit. The space between the hedges was too close to take flight, too tall to see over. A place of trickery she realized, as some paths led to dead ends.

She tried to retrace her steps but quickly became lost before she stumbled across the most shocking thing.

The starlight provided enough illumination for her to recognize Michelina, wearing a short robe, made shorter on one side as she'd hiked it above her waist to better wrap her leg around a bigger angel's waist. She moaned as if in pain, and yet she appeared to be participating in whatever it was that hurt. What were they doing? Why were they naked below the waist and banging their groins against each other?

It came to her suddenly! The rite of fornication. What do you know? Opposing male and female parts did fit!

Michelina cried out, screamed really, and clawed at the angel moving rapidly against her.

The poor thing! She was in pain. Helen couldn't stand by and do nothing, so she yelled, "Leave her alone!"

The male angel's eyes widened, but it was Michelina who hissed, "She can't tell anyone."

The male angel tugged his robe over a penis much larger than Helen had ever seen. She usually dealt with cherubs.

Distracted by the angel's massive protuberance, it took her a moment to realize he'd drawn a sword from his hip and pulled it back to swing.

Helen squeaked. "What are you doing?" Was she about to be killed? She wasn't the one who'd broken any laws.

"Don't you use that sword." Michelina came to her rescue.

Helen almost sighed in relief.

"You can't do it here," Michelina chided. "Think of the blood. Do it somewhere else. Somewhere we won't get caught."

The implication widened Helen's eyes.

"I'll take her below," said the angel.

Where below? Helen glanced at her feet. There was nothing under there but—

The angel lunged for her, and she yelled, which led to Michelina hissing, "Shh."

"I will not shush!" Helen yelped as she struggled against the male angel. "Help. They're breaking—"

A hand slammed over her mouth.

Helen bit it. The angel yelled before thumping her temple with a fist. The next thing she knew, she woke in someone's arms, head throbbing.

She blinked and slurred, "Whaaat happened?"

"Don't move. We're almost there." The deep voice and its claim didn't reassure.

Her head ached with pain, not something she'd often experienced. She only rarely hurt herself.

A jolt ended their flight, and the angel holding her let go. She hit the ground with a sharp cry, her palms slapping against stone that felt pitted and slimy.

She blinked and gaped and made the mistake of sucking in a breath. Putrid. Awful. Stomach clenching. She gagged. "What's that smell?"

"Welcome to Earth."

4

HANDS THRUST INTO HIS POCKETS, Julio strolled the sidewalk. Others might drive to work or take the public transit system, but he quite enjoyed the exercise. The ambiance helped, too. Life teemed around him with sights and smells, which weren't always pleasant, but it beat the never-ending ash falling in Hell.

Not so long ago, Julio had been living at Grim Headquarters, a gloomy castle-like structure in Hell where he awaited his assignments—the collection of souls. But given the Canadian guild never had much work, the Dark Lord had reassigned them to Earth as part of a new initiative called Grim Dating. Julio had gone from reaper to pimp.

At least it came with all the cable channels.

As he strode past an alley, a place where he'd done more than one deal back in his living days, he felt a tug on his cloak. *The* cloak. The one all the reapers wore because of their deal with the devil. Die and become one of the damned or serve as a guide for souls when death claimed their fleshy shell.

Everyone went to Hell. Even the supposedly virtuous. Apparently, protests and veganism weren't enough to wipe clean their sins. He'd never once in his career brought anyone to Heaven. Although he'd heard of some souls being lost to Limbo, spirits that somehow never met up with a Reaper or who refused to be corralled. Their loss, as Limbo tended to eat at them, whittling away at their souls until there was nothing but an echo left.

Julio tugged at the smoke-like fabric of his cloak, only it remained stiff as if caught on something, rigid and at attention despite nothing being there. Nothing but a feeling, the kind he used to get when assigned a reaping mission. Except he was a dating specialist now. He no longer chased after death.

Still, the sense of urgency couldn't be denied. His grim magic wanted him to go down the alley. Therefore, he did. It wasn't as if he had anything to fear. Humans very rarely went around with swords, decapitating people, and he would heal from pretty much any other wound. However, not being keen on pain, he did approach with stealth. Once he turned the corner, he'd leave the faint light of the street for pure shadow.

His cloak rose to swirl around him, covering him head to toe as he stepped around the edge and perceived an odd sight.

A woman was huddled on the ground, curly hair spilling over her shoulders, hand raised, her mouth rounded in surprise and horror, given the sword held over her head by a massive dude. "Please," she beseeched.

The man remained impassive, and for a second, Julio saw ghostly wings at his back. Holy fuck, the sword dude was an angel about to mete out divine retribution.

Julio hesitated. The rules were clear. Don't engage with angels.

Ever.

And she was also definitely an angel. The more she shivered, the more her wings took shape and substance at her back, but it was the flickering halo that cinched it.

Her lip trembled as she said, "Don't kill me. I promise to not tell."

Big Angel sneered. "The dead don't speak."

Not entirely true. Damned souls had lots to say, but Julio couldn't be sure about angels, so as the sword began its descent, despite it being none of his business, he sprang forward. His cloak snapped, revealing him stepping out of the shadows. His silver-hued stave emerged, halting the glowing blade with a scream of metal and shower of sparks.

"You dare!" boomed the angel as he whirled on Julio.

"You gotta admit, this isn't exactly sporting. Aren't angels all about honor?"

"She is a criminal," Big Angel declared.

"Am not!" Little Angel hotly retorted, pushing to her knees.

Julio's gaze briefly flicked in her direction, and Big Angel pounced, sword swinging. Julio only just managed to parry the strokes.

"Show your face, taker of souls," hissed the angel.

As if Julio would pause long enough to take off his cloak, his only shield. "Why? So you can see how much prettier I am than you?"

"Argh!" The angel swung his sword. Julio parried with his stave. While that distracted the angel, Julio punched. *Snap. Crack.*

The white tunic wore a spray of blood. What do you know; angels bled red.

"How dare you!" Big Angel reeled, holding his face.

"Don't pull the self-righteous crap with me. You were going to murder an unarmed woman."

"Reapers are supposed to be neutral parties," retorted the angel.

"If it makes you feel better, I won't let her kill you either."

The woman snorted.

"This is Heaven's business," Big Angel pompously informed.

"Only until you bring death into it, and according to my reaper handbook, she's not due."

"She will die and so will you!" The angel charged at him, expression fierce, and Julio only just managed to stay ahead of the blows.

He dropped to his haunches and swung his stave, the blow glancing off the angel's ankle. Big Angel yelled and stumbled, but when Julio would have pressed his advantage, the angel sprang into the air and grabbed hold of a fire escape, climbing quickly until he stood a few stories overhead. He jumped off with a mighty push of his wings yelling, "This isn't over, reaper. You will wish you'd walked away."

"Up yours, asshole." Julio flipped the angel off. Why not? He'd already gone to Hell, and it wasn't all that bad.

With the fuckwad gone, Julio made his way to the dazed woman, who, under better control, had tucked away her wings and halo. She didn't appear ready to move.

He prodded her. "Come on, Curls. Get up. Get moving. You can't stick around. I'm pretty sure you don't want to be here when the asshole returns with some of his buddies."

"Here?" She blinked at him. "Where is here? He said Earth."

"Yup. Canada to be exact."

"That's impossible." She touched the pavement and rose to her feet, looking around. "I can't be on Earth."

"Guess again."

"You don't understand. I don't belong here. I have to return to Heaven. Which way are the gates?" She whirled as if she could see the pearly impossibilities. Only those allowed entry knew their location.

He stared at her. "You're an angel. Don't you have like a homing device for home?"

She shook her head. "I've never been outside the nursery, and I was unconscious when he kidnapped me. I must return. You have to show me the way."

Julio hated to burst her naïve bubble. "Sorry, Curls, but short of you dying and living a perfect life, the only place you're going is a lot hotter."

5

"I AM NOT GOING TO HELL!" Helen squealed, mostly in shock. Had she damned herself? She'd not meant for her restless feet to get her condemned.

"Seems logical given you appear to have fallen."

"I am not...That is..." She bit her lip. He might have a point. She'd broken the rules and now found herself far from home.

"Why was that angel trying to smite you? Aren't you guys all about love and peace?" he asked.

"Obviously he was seduced by the devil. Why else would he attack me?" Her mind still had a hard time grasping what had happened.

"He was obviously worried about something. Did you catch him being bad?"

"I did! Him and Michelina." It emerged hot and indignant. "They were fraternizing. Indulging in the rite of fornication!" Her cheeks warmed.

"You caught them fucking? That's not a big deal. People fuck all the time. Or was he married?"

"Is fucking another word for fornication?" she asked, unfamiliar with the term.

"Um. Er. More like a slang word for it. Have you never heard anyone cussing in Heaven?"

"Cursing is against the rules. As is fraternization and killing."

"How many rules do you have to follow?"

"At last count? One hundred and eleven thousand four hundred and sixty-three. But I heard they'd be adding four more soon." The latest ban being for a fruit called pineapple on something called a pizza. An Earth thing, obviously, so she wasn't sure how it applied in Heaven.

"Did you say over one hundred thousand? That's fucking insane. And you obey every single one?"

"Usually. Except for tonight." Her head drooped. "I just wanted to go for a walk."

"And saw something you shouldn't." He sighed. "Sorry for your luck." He actually sounded sincere, although it was hard to tell given his cloak swirled around him still, hiding his features, concealing him. Yet she wasn't scared.

"I need to return to Heaven and explain. Accept my punishment for leaving my room after sundown."

"What makes you think that angel won't kill you if you try?"

"Because that's evil!" she huffed.

"You do realize he tried to take your head off with his oversized knife?"

"He was trying to scare me." And he'd succeeded.

"He would have killed you if I'd not stepped in,

37

Curls. You're a witness to him being bad. He won't want you coming back to Heaven."

Much as she hated to wrap her mind around it, she knew he spoke the truth. "I'll find a way."

"Does that way involve waiting here for him?"

"I should change locations."

"Yes, you should. You got a place to go?"

She opened and shut her mouth before admitting, "No."

"I might know a few places, Curls. Let's boogie." Snaring her hand, he tugged her out of the alley into a busy thoroughfare that had her flinching at the stimulation overdose.

Lights.

Noise.

People.

Humans!

Holy Father who art imprisoned in heaven. Real humans. She could tell because none of them had shadow wings or halos.

"Um, you might not want to say that out loud, angel," her rescuer murmured, drawing his arm around her shoulders and tucking her into the pocket of swirling darkness that flowed from his shoulders.

"I've never seen any before. They look quite…" She paused, only to blurt out, "Ordinary."

He chuckled. "You mean, like you?"

"Not entirely. They don't have wings or halos." She glanced at him. "Neither do you, and yet you're not like them. What are you?" Because while he didn't sport extra parts, he did have a cloak at his back that undulated like smoke and kept his face hidden.

At her query, he finally shoved back his hood and she saw a solid man with a jaw bearing a shadow of facial hair. "I'm a reaper. Name of Julio. And you are?"

"Helen," she muttered in reply as she eyed Julio. "Nursery nanny in Heaven."

"Lucky babies."

She blinked, not quite sure what he meant and eyed him more closely. "When you say you're a reaper, do you mean a grim reaper, the monsters who steal souls?"

He chuckled. "We don't steal, just guide them to their final destination."

"Hell," she stated.

"If that's their fate, then yes."

"I was taught you were at least twice our height with great big swords to cleave our souls from our bodies." She slashed a hand.

"Sorry to disappoint."

She wasn't. He actually pleased the eye. She felt heat in her cheeks again and eyed the ground as they walked. "Given that we are not supposed to see death coming, does this mean since I have that you're here to take my soul?" Did she have a soul? Wasn't that a human thing?

"If I wanted you dead, I wouldn't have saved you."

"I suppose not. I'm very confused, and I don't like this at all. I just want to go back to Heaven."

"Afraid you're stuck, Curls. But it's not all bad. Earth's got some cool shit to offer. I mean, um, stuff."

Curls? Her hand went to her hair. She'd never had a nickname before. Or was it because he'd forgotten her proper one already?

"What would I do here? Would the humans assign me a home?"

"Only if you pay rent. Which means money."

"You mean riches?" She pursed her lips. "I have nothing. Material possessions are for the covetous."

"You don't own anything? Knickknacks? Books?"

"I have a Bible in my room."

"So you own something."

She shook her head. "I borrowed it from the library." Shelves of the same seven repeating books.

"Well, on Earth, people like to own stuff. And to buy it, you need money, which means you'll have to get a job."

Her expression brightened. "I can work."

"Most places will want identification." He frowned at her. "I don't usually deal in that department."

"I have identification. My face and name." Each one was unique in Heaven. Except when it came to rare twins. If too identical, they got numbered. Like Manfred One and Manfred Two, cherubs that recently graduated from the nursery.

"That's not enough. You need plastic. Like this." He pulled something from a pocket and showed her a slim card with his image and writing on it.

"This is a horrible picture." She pointed. "Doesn't look like you at all."

"Yeah, but that's what they want you to carry

around. To prove who you are. You need one to get a job and open a bank account for direct deposit."

"What's a bank?"

His lips flattened. "You have a lot to learn, Curls."

Helen frowned. "Surely it can't be that difficult." After all, humans managed it. "I will provide my services as a nanny and receive a room and sustenance."

Julio rubbed a hand over his jaw. "Wow, you really have no clue. Do you realize there are millions of people living in this city?"

"Millions?" The very concept floored her. Heaven didn't have that many living in it. Then again, what did she know? She knew nothing outside of the nursery. Tonight had proven she was woefully lacking in education.

"Yes, millions. That many people in one concentrated area means there's competition for jobs and housing. For someone like you with no skills, no proper identification, who needs to hide..." He whistled. "You might have been better off dying. In Hell, all that shit is taken care of for you." He slipped and didn't correct his swearing.

"I don't belong in Hell."

"It's so cute when angels deny the truth." It wasn't Julio that replied to her statement but a stranger who suddenly appeared, bringing with him the most obnoxious smell. However, that wasn't what drew her attention.

Older than Julio, the male stood a few inches shorter and definitely not as wide, yet he took up more space as if his body couldn't quite contain him. Heat spilled from the man's frame. It blurred the edges of his shape, making her imagine giant leathery wings and curling horns.

Upon seeing the flames dancing in his eyes, Helen did the sign of the cross and screamed, "It's the devil!"

6

THE NINTH CIRCLE DISAPPEARED OVERNIGHT, and no one noticed until the morning. But once the Hellwork got wind...

It was everywhere. HellBC. *The New Hell Times.* Hellbook. The titles accompanying the articles varied only slightly.

"Dark Lord Losing His Grip Along With the Ninth Ring."

"Is This the End of Hell As We Know It?"

The Antifa, sent to hell during a purge after their last round of rioting, began a campaign in the seventh ring that involved defunding the legion. Joke was on them. The legion worked for free. But a perk of the job was they got to pound on the Antifa agitators and take all their things. After all, sharing was equitable.

But the underlying message was Lucifer's minions, damned and demon alike, were losing faith in him. And he didn't know how to stop it.

Gaia patted him on the back. "There, there, Luc. If

the rings get devoured and your kingdom disappears, you can always live in my garden."

The Garden of Eden, with all its healthy growing things where he'd have almost no power. Where Lucifer would be a lesser demon relying on his wife to survive. It was beyond emasculating.

"Shouldn't you be worried? What if this thing comes after you next?" he snapped.

"Testy, testy. Did Jujube keep you up last night?"

"Our daughter is a demanding wench, just like her mother." She'd insisted they care for their progeny themselves. Didn't Gaia remember how tending them would lead to liking them? Liking them always made it harder to kill them later on when they betrayed him.

So far, Muriel was almost thirty and still not interested in his throne, but of late, he had to wonder about his oldest living child, Bambi. She'd gone from biddable to confident with authority. Never a good sign. Plus, he kept hearing rumors she was seeing someone. But who? Because War's armor was rusting with the tears he'd shed after being jilted.

Lucifer didn't like being in the dark. He also didn't like being made a fool. Which was why, after his wife's offer, he stood on the edge of the eighth ring, within inches of the border, and did his best to sound confidant and reassuring to the crowd as he said, "I am sure that, whatever is happening out there in the Wilds, we needn't worry. Think of it as our dimension adjusting to recent drops in numbers." Blah. Blah. Blah. He spun them a line of bullshit that could almost be believed.

Numbers were down, and the kingdom was resizing so as to not waste space.

Some people swallowed the lie. Others saw the holes in his explanation. Especially the older demons and beings who remembered the emptiness of Hell after the hundred-year war with Heaven. Whole neighborhoods went quiet, and yet they'd not lost a single foot of any ring. What was different this time?

Lucifer dressed casually in his new jumpsuit so as not to appear worried. The material was covered in fanged and evil pineapples chewing on people. Like a tri-dimensional image, as he shifted so did the images, so it appeared as if they truly were grinding up bones and flesh. Usually his outfits were a crowd pleaser. Only the damned and demonic didn't admire him this time but rather remained riveted by the fog. It didn't help that every so often someone suddenly ran past him to be swallowed by the mist.

"Nothing to worry about," Lucifer said. His words fell on frightened, deaf ears.

"Why haven't you fixed it? Are you scared?" someone dared to ask.

Lucifer would have smitten them, but the damned couldn't exactly be killed. Tortured yes, but only the pit could recycle the dead souls that ended up in his kingdom.

A demon made it worse by saying, "Don't question the Dark Lord's plan."

Lucifer only wished he had a fucking plan that didn't involve stepping into that fog. He could swear it taunted him. Dared him to enter. Teased him.

"Yellow-bellied coward."

Wait, that was a damned one calling him a yellow belly. He turned his glare on Lester, a guy who used to swindle women out of money when they brought their cars in for repair. He'd served his time but remained a dick. A snap of Lucifer's fingers sent Lester for further punishment, but the insult remained.

Lucifer steeled himself, ready to show them all he didn't fear by walking into the mist, when Bambi appeared.

"Dark Lord!" she called to him. "A moment of your time."

He stifled his relief as he replied, "I'm terribly busy."

"I know. Apologies." She even dipped into a curtsy so respectful with her eyes downcast it made him sick until she shot him a sly glance through her lashes. "It is a matter of urgency, your excellency."

"Then let's make haste. I'll be back later for this," he declared as he snapped his fingers and brought the two of them back to his castle.

"Looks like I rescued you in time," she said the moment they arrived.

"I'm not a coward." The devil feared nothing except his wife on a rampage.

"I must have misread the situation. If you'd like to return and check out that mist, my news can wait."

He glared. "You lied about the urgency?"

"Well duh. I had to since I didn't want you going into that fog. As a matter of fact, I'd recommend staying far away. We can't afford to lose you." Her concern made him frown until she added, "Hell must have a leader so no doing anything rash before we have a proper replacement." For a while, he thought he had a son who would challenge him, but Chris—raised to believe he was the antichrist—turned out to be Elyon's indiscretion.

"As if anyone could take my place," Lucifer blustered, ignoring the fact he finally had a true son. A cute little helpless thing. They choked so easily at this age. Who knew, maybe the little shit might even live long enough to try and mutiny against his Father.

If his mother didn't kill him first. Good news was she appeared to be over her postpartum depression and just in time. He'd been worried she'd heard about the rumors that Jujube would kill her and take her place. But after a few tense moments, where he'd snared his wife's wrist as she held a knife over the crib, and the time he'd caught her tossing Jujube into the pond, she appeared to have adjusted to motherhood.

Bambi snapped her fingers. "Yoohoo. Hell to Lucifer. I lost you there for a second. You okay?"

"Never better. Although I could do without this sudden fake affection you're showing me. What is the real reason you came to get me?"

"Because I thought you'd want to hear the news. Heaven's on high alert. Apparently, an angel has gone missing after committing a boatload of sins. Presumed to have escaped to Earth."

"Really?" His expression brightened. He rubbed his hands and said, "This I've got to see!"

7

THE DEVIL SMILED AT HELEN. He was a charming thing with dimples that made him more handsome than he should be.

"I see you've heard of me." Lucifer sounded quite pleased. "All bad, I hope."

"The worst!" Helen exclaimed.

"You flatterer." The demon actually pretended to be abashed.

It seemed her insults catered to his evil ego. "Begone, foul thing. You have no power over me." She held her fingers in a cross like she'd been taught.

The devil sighed. "Seriously? Thousands of years and they remain idiots."

Even Julio appeared incredulous as he exclaimed, "What the fuck was that supposed to do?"

Feeling a tad foolish, Helen shrugged. "Everyone knows the symbol of the cross keeps evil at bay."

"Who the fuck told you that?" Julio asked.

Her shoulders rounded. "It is common knowledge that Lucifer fears the Lord's holy cross."

That made the devil snort smoke. "I can't believe that useless crap is still being taught. But your lack of proper education isn't why I'm here. Apparently, you've been a bad angel, Helen." He shook a finger at her, the ring on it etched into some kind of monster head with winking bright green eyes. It matched the green on his satin pants and vest. He didn't appear as she'd imagined.

Her teachers had described the devil as a massive monster with horns and hooves. Evil in his gaze. Not a dimple in his cheek. Or a flower in his buttonhole.

"I am not bad. I did nothing wrong," she said, defending her innocence.

"Lie!" the devil yelled.

She flushed. "Only a little one. I admit to walking outside after curfew."

The devil made a noise. "They wouldn't have condemned you for wandering after dark. According to the warrant for your capture, it's much worse."

"Warrant?" She knew what they were. After all, Heaven sometimes had troublemakers.

The devil snapped his fingers, and her image appeared. Her name written underneath, along with a listing of her crimes.

"Being sought for the subversion of cherubs. Illegal association with humans. The smuggling of banned items from the Hell plane." Her voice raised in pitch with each ridiculous claim. "I didn't do anything on that list."

"Truth!" The devil wrinkled his nose. "Ugh. That did not feel good."

"Someone is making false accusation against her?" Julio asked.

"Apparently someone is mad at little Helen here. What'd you do? Piss in their cereal? Short sheet their bed? This is Heaven. Maybe you forgot to say a prayer a thousand times every single day."

"No. Never." She sought to follow the devil's rapid-fire speech and the accusations he made. How dare Lucifer accuse her of wrongdoing? Her only crime was walking outside. It didn't deserve this punishment, especially given what she'd seen others doing.

"Doesn't matter what you did," Julio pointed out. "The fact of the matter is someone is angry enough they're pulling out all the stops to ensure you don't make it back to Heaven."

"This is because of Michelina and the angel she was..." She trailed off, unable to repeat the blasphemy she'd seen with the devil leering in anticipation.

"Go on, Helen. Tell us what you saw. In detail. Lots of detail." Lucifer rubbed his hands.

"No. What they were doing was a sin. And once I expose them, everyone will see the lies being told about me and know I'm innocent."

Lucifer barked with laughter. "So naïve. From the sounds of it, you caught one of the Archangels fucking. And they are not people you want to cross."

"Angels do not fornicate. Only humans and animals do."

Again, the devil laughed. "The dumb is strong in

you, but I digress. My babies won't sleep for much longer, which means I need to finish this conversation. There is a warrant for your arrest."

"Let them arrest me, then. I shall prove my innocence." She lifted her chin.

The Dark Lord turned to Julio and said, "Is she really that dumb?"

The reaper shrugged. "It would seem so." He then turned to her and said slowly, "I highly doubt you'll make it to Heaven alive if you turn yourself in."

"Someone wants you dead, dear Helen, and that is a problem," the devil stated. "Currently, you are too good for Hell, but Heaven doesn't want you either. Meaning, if you die, you'll end up in Limbo."

"The nothing place." A shiver went through her.

"What can she do to avoid that?" Julio asked.

"It would only take a little sinning to join the most awesome club in the universe. Become one of my minions and you'll live forever, short of severe injury or decapitation."

"I don't want to be a demon." The very idea horrified.

"Oh, you wouldn't be a demon. But I have plenty of positions perfect for a fallen angel."

"I won't become a citizen of Hell." She lifted her chin. "I am wrongly accused. I will prove my innocence and return to Heaven."

For some reason both Julio and the devil laughed, hard enough the Dark Lord wiped his eyes.

"Oh, goodness, you're a rare one. An angel with a sense of humor. Love it. Wish I could stay and chuckle some more, but duty calls. Julio, I want you to take special care of Helen for me."

A puzzled expression creased Julio's face. "You want me to reap her soul?"

"Only if someone does manage to kill her. Otherwise, the poor girl needs a guide in this world."

"I'm not a teacher," he growled.

"Never say never. I've had some of my finest orgasms with eager pupils." With a wink and a snap of his fingers, the devil disappeared.

But the offer he'd made to become one of his evil minions lingered like the sulfur stench of him.

Never.

8

"WELL, THAT WAS FUN."

Not.

Julio had gotten used to the devil popping in at the Grim Dating office, but by himself? That was a first. And then to assign him cultural duties with an angel who redefined stubborn? Like fuck.

"You serve the Dark Lord," she stated.

"Yeah, but only because no one else will touch us. Your boss up there pretends we don't exist. Angels tend to give us the cold shoulder, too. Limbo is still leaderless. The Dark Lord ensures we have a home and a purpose."

"Seems a dark purpose to me."

He shrugged. "Death is only dark if you see it as the end. For many, it's a new beginning."

"When angels die, we become part of our Father, who is resting in Heaven."

"If you say so." And then because he couldn't help himself, "Do you really think Elyon is your Father?"

"As much as you know the devil is yours."

"The devil isn't my dad. My dad was a piece of shit who beat me. My mom worked three jobs and dropped dead of a heart attack. I was an asshole while alive. When I died, the devil offered a chance to become something better. A reaper." Lucifer had given Julio a job with purpose.

"And that was a good thing?"

He smiled. "Fuck yeah, it was. I became less of an asshole."

"Well, our Father, who created Heaven, made me. Makes everyone."

"Not everyone. Humans fornicate, remember?" He winked as he reminded her.

She blushed. It was really too cute. She bit her lip. "Not angels."

"Then how are you made?"

"I don't know. Do you?" The query was much too eager.

He frowned. "How can you not know? Don't angels have sex and pop out babies like everyone else?" Even demons procreated that way.

"No!" she hotly exclaimed, her cheeks bright red. "Babies arrive by stork. No one seems to know where they come from."

"Stork?" The ridiculousness of it almost had him laughing until he saw her serious expression. "Fuck me, they really do exist? I thought the stork thing was a myth."

The shake of her head sent her curls dancing. "It's true. Cherubs arrive by stork."

"From where?"

Her shoulders rolled. "I don't know. Although I did know another nanny who said something about cabbage patches."

"The doll?" he asked. Weren't they a fad in the eighties or nineties?

She pursed her lips. "Dolls are the devil's toys."

The very fact she believed it filled him with pity. "Oh, Curls. You've got so much to learn."

"Not from you, I don't. I won't do the devil's bidding." She lifted her chin.

"You're gonna conquer the world on your own?"

"I don't need to conquer. I shall have truth as my sword. My integrity as my shield."

His steps slowed as they reached the offices of Grim Dating. "You think you can do this on your own, then I guess this is where we part ways, Curls. If you change your mind and need me, call." He flipped out a card and pressed it into her hand. "Good luck."

"You're leaving?"

"Yup. That's my office. Sure you don't want my help settling in?"

"Never, demonic minion!"

He snorted. "Suit yourself." With a wave, Julio left her and crossed the street.

He could have sworn he felt her staring between the shoulder blades. An incredible urge filled him to turn around to march right back. She was too innocent to be wandering around on her own. Innocent being another word for dumb. She'd probably end up mugged or worse within the hour.

Not his problem. If it was her time, nothing he did could change that. The *Final Destination* movies had gotten that part right. Only it wasn't an invisible force that made sure order was kept but a squad of Death Marines who appeared out of nowhere and left as eerily, the human shell dead, the soul bound and gagged for Hell.

The devil ordered me to teach her. Couldn't teach someone who wouldn't listen.

Still, the reminder of his orders had him turning around to glance back at Helen, only to realize she'd left already. How long before she either ended up dead or called the number on the card?

Entering the Grim Dating headquarters, he barely noticed the slick chrome and marble. Everything was brand spanking new and ash free. He had to admit he liked the new digs and the perks. Earth-side, he got to enjoy everything from food to music to the amenities that didn't always work so well in Hell, like kick-ass sound systems and video games.

More than a few mommas' basement-dwelling darlings got a shock when they arrived in Hell to discover their slovenly, lazy behavior meant an eternity of working the slop jobs and at the end of their shift? Sixty-nine channels of nothing on the Hell-tube.

The angel he'd met would have her entire world-view rattled. He'd heard of living a sheltered life. Apparently, it didn't compare with a brain-washed, heavenly resident.

Julio waved hello to security as he made his way to

the top floor with the executive offices. Because hell yeah, he'd made executive. He even had a door with his name. Field Operation Manager being his formal title. Mostly, he made sure the demons and denizens from Hell that were brought Earth-side for hookups behaved, and if they didn't? He dragged them in kicking and screaming, sometimes with their pants still around their ankles.

The receptionist, wearing tight serpentine curls and slanted cat-eye glasses, sat at the curved reception desk and offered him a smile. "Julio, what a coincidence. The commander is here and wants to speak with you."

"What's he doing here this late at night?" Brody usually preferred to keep daytime hours, whereas Julio liked to switch them up.

"He popped in to handle something. Wanted to set up a meeting for tomorrow but given you're here..."

"I'll go see what he wants then." Julio strode quickly across the carpeted floor, a slate gray that complemented the other shades of gray that decorated the place. Grim Dating didn't have gimmicky hearts and cupids like other matchmaking places. They took their business seriously. Except on their merchandise. The cartoon reaper with his scythe stabbing a heart was turning out to be a big hit. They couldn't keep the bumper stickers or T-shirts in stock.

The glass door set inside a frosted wall led into a lush vestibule for the big man's office. Brody, the commander, and Posie, recently appointed partner—and Brody's pregnant, eating-everything-in-sight fiancée—were standing in front of the secretary's desk rather than inside the office with its panoramic view.

Bambi, the devil's own daughter, sat in the secretarial seat, twirling around. She wore a skirt that actually reached her knees, ankle boots, and a blouse tucked into the waistband and not cropped under her breasts. She almost looked mature.

Then she saw him and winked, offering the most lascivious smile possible. "There's that hunk of Latino burning love we wanted to see. Wearing way too many clothes, I should add."

"You can't say that," Posie chastised. "It can be construed as sexual harassment."

"You're ruining my fun. Do you know how long I've waited to be in charge so I can use my position of power to demand favors from people?" Bambi pouted. "Besides, I was just telling the truth from a position of experience."

"And for it to be harassment, it has to be unwelcome. The CEO of Grim Dating can compliment me any day." Julio winked but didn't worry about Bambi taking him up on the offer. Rumor had it she was getting serious with someone. Love appeared to be in the air, and contagious. He'd been taking extra vitamins to avoid getting contaminated.

"Ugh, now I remember why I avoid coming here. Such spoilsports. Why did you call me, anyhow?" Bambi complained.

Brody slung his arm around Posie's waist. "We're going on a trip."

"And you wanted to invite me along to spice things up?" Bambi's expression brightened.

"No!" Posie and Brody exclaimed as one. They did that every so often. If they kept it up, they'd end up with a cutesy name like Brosie. Maybe Pody?

"Just the two of you? Sounds dull to me, but hey, whatever floats your boat." Bambi rose, readying to leave.

"Wait." Brody held up a hand. "I called you both to talk about delegation of duties while I'm gone. Julio, you'll be my eyes and ears but only report if it's something I need to know or deal with. Bambi, I figured you'd take our spot."

"Work here? On Earth?" Bambi's nose wrinkled. "No thanks. I'm enjoying the break. Make him do it." She pointed.

"Me?" Julio exclaimed. "Oh no. Spying I can do, but I am not management material."

"Meaning you won't try and steal my job," Brody mused aloud. "You know what, that just might work. Julio, you're in charge."

Having seen what Brody dealt with on a daily basis, Julio roughly shook his head. "You can't do this to me. I'm not meant to be fettered to a desk."

"It's only for two weeks."

"Two weeks!" His voice reached a pitched he'd not heard since his teenage years.

"Yeah, two weeks. Try not to screw it up."

He'd try. He really would. But it didn't help that the moment Brody left, and Julio was in charge, the devil appeared wearing an evil grin.

"Hello, Julio. Miss me?"

"I saw you less than fifteen minutes ago."

"And already disobeying I see. Where's the angel?"

"Off proving she doesn't need me."

"Fear not. She'll be back. In the meantime, I've got a special job for you."

Was it just him that heard the ominous music?

9

"Grab her, would you?" Lucifer held out his daughter. "I need both hands to show you something." His cute baby girl was dressed in a custom pink romper covered in hungry piranhas. Adorable.

Julio eyed him with trepidation. As Jujube reached for him, the reaper recoiled as if she were about to go off like a bomb. A possibility. Jujube did so love her temper tantrums. Lucifer had to reinforce her crib a few times.

"If I must." With a long-suffering sigh, Julio plucked the baby and held her to his chest, hand holding her head, arm tucked under her bottom. A pro.

Lucifer frowned. "You're awfully comfortable with her. How is that possible given I don't recall any bastards in your file?" Because he'd been looking for any illegal progeny that might be able to join his legion.

"I was second oldest of seven kids. And two of my sisters got pregnant in their teens."

A reminder Julio came from a long line of sinners.

His family practically had a seat reserved on Charon's boat, given how many of them died every year. But good news, they procreated like crazy. For example, Julio only knew of six siblings, yet by Lucifer's reckoning, Daddy had sprinkled at least five more.

"I will keep your experience in mind the next time the missus and I need a night out. Crazy how no one wants to spend time with the prettiest girl in the world. Yes, she is." Lucifer chucked her chin, and Jujube giggled. Not her real name, but the one that stuck. Lucifer kept her real name hidden, even from Gaia. There was something still not right about his wife.

Too happy. Too bright. Too horny.

All that sex he'd been having lately. The BJs... He didn't trust it one bit. Married sex was supposed to be begged for. Then indulged in between commercial breaks. Maybe a quickie in the shower. But instead his babies slept at least a few hours straight and Gaia had been showing up wearing different outfits each time.

She was definitely up to something. Which was why he fucked her, and he fucked her good. Maybe he'd fuck her hard enough she'd admit her plan.

Okay, he fucked her just because it was amazing. But still, there had to be a way to get her to talk to him. Let him peek inside her head and see what she plotted.

"Why do you need two hands?" Julio interrupted, having placed the baby on his lap facing him so he could make faces at her.

The jealousy when she giggled and clapped almost had him erasing Julio. Stealing his girl! DIE!

Wait. He needed the guy still.

"Ah yes, the reason I'm here." Lucifer pulled a cigar from his jacket stained in baby milk. With his other hand he lit it with a Zippo engraved with a duck, in loving memory of his rubber one, which had to be tossed after a toxic incident in the bath with his son.

May your duckie soul float forever. He'd miss its jabby horns when he sat down without looking and it rammed him in the butt.

Fun times.

"You shouldn't smoke around the baby," Julio admonished.

The nerve. Taking the devil to task. Lucifer slapped a gag over Julio's mouth. "The grownups are talking. Meaning me. So listen. That angel you met."

Julio's head inclined, and he rolled his shoulders in a universal *what?*

"She's cute."

Julio snorted and rolled his eyes.

"Yes, she sounds a little crazy. But one can't really blame her given her upbringing."

Julio waggled his brows. Lucifer couldn't quite understand his question and removed the gag. "You wanted to say something?"

"A little crazy? She doesn't know how angels are made."

"Do *you* know how angels are made?" Lucifer asked.

For a second, Julio's mouth worked. "Aren't they made the same way as everyone else?"

"Not according to Heaven. According to them, baby angels just appear, brought there magically by storks."

"Wait, are you telling me that bullshit story she told

me is true?" His brows rose. "A fucking stork. Where does the bird get them from?"

Lucifer shrugged. "They don't teach that part in Heaven."

"But you know," Julio stated.

"Of course, I know where babies come from," Lucifer exclaimed. "However, if I just tell the angel, she'll think I'm lying."

"Show her proof."

"Are you saying I should have sex with her and impregnate her with my virile seed?" He waited for Gaia to react. Not a single jealous lightning strike.

"Uh, no?"

"I'm married, I'll have you know," Lucifer huffed, feeling a little jilted. Did Gaia simply not care anymore? Or was she stepping out on him?

He'd kill anyone who laid a hand on his wife.

No, killing was too gentle. He'd torture them for an eternity. Muahahahaha.

As he laughed out loud, both Julio and Jujube eyeballed him.

"You okay, Dark Lord?"

"Yes! Never better. Anyhow, on to your mission. I need you to educate the angel. Although, FYI, she's a virgin."

A massive coughing fit had the baby bobbling on Julio's lap. "You want to me to…"

Lucifer chuckled. "As if I'd ever ask one of my loyal employees to have sex with someone. It would be completely up to you whether you'd like to pop a cherry." Julio turned a color that appeared unhealthy.

Lucifer grabbed his baby. "Are you going to puke? Because I just had these boots licked and shone with a thousand tears from a repentant asshole."

"Why do you want Helen to know how babies are made?"

"Because she and other angels are being lied to. Oppressed by my brother and his ancient beliefs that are sexist to females."

"And telling them how babies are made fixes this how?" Julio asked.

"Because then they'd be sinning, according to my brother, and they'd fall. All mine without lifting a hand or killing anyone. Elegant, eh?"

"You think if angels have sex Heaven will collapse?"

No, or it would have happened already, but Lucifer wasn't about to tell his minion. "It won't collapse, but it will precipitate an uprising." Because Lucifer had seen a few futures where Heaven erupted into chaos.

"And this uprising all rests on Helen knowing how babies are made?" Such skepticism in Julio's tone.

"Not just babies. Angel babies. She needs to meet the Nephilim living on this plane." And in case Julio didn't know what that meant, he explained. "Nephilim are angel-human mixed children."

"They exist?"

"Well, duh. Haven't you been paying attention? Angels have been fucking and making babies with humans since they ventured down from Heaven."

"Wouldn't that render them sinners and automatically make them fall?"

"Except for the fact no sex with humans means they

die out," Lucifer answered before Julio's slow brain caught up. "You see my brother learned early on that reproducing in a very limited gene pool proved less than ideal. So, he outright banned sex in Heaven. Made it a sin and sterilized half the population."

Julio figured it out quickly this time. "He sterilized the females, because even if they do have sex, the lack of pregnancy means there's no proof to expose the lie."

"Now you understand. Boy angels, as a reward for being brown-nosing sycophants, get to flock down to Earth and sprinkle their seed. Those born with wings are taken to Heaven."

"I've never heard of a baby born with wings."

"Of course not. Humans can't see them. Which you should know. Their wings are like your cloaks when on Earth."

Julio bounced the baby as he took on a pensive expression. "I find it hard to believe angels have been using humans as baby makers and I've never heard of it."

"As if my brother would allow such a thing to come to light. This has been an elaborate plot of his for eons."

"Who's got a plot?" Lucifer hadn't noticed his wife had arrived.

"Wench, what a delight to see you!"

Gaia appeared in fine form, her hair bound back in French braids, her summer dress light and airy, floating around on gossamer wings. The butterflies were too delighted about being near Mother Earth to scream about being used for fashion.

"Husband. You are looking fine." Her gaze tracked

down over him, and he shivered. Such wicked promise in that gaze.

"I was just talking to Julio here about my plan to destabilize Heaven." Close to the truth but skirting it.

Gaia should have called him out. Instead she smiled. "I can't wait to hear all about it. First, my little girl needs a bath." Gaia held out her hands for the baby.

"She had one this morning after an incident while diaper changing."

"Then we'll snuggle." The fingers that reached elongated, vine-like and grasping.

Lucifer snatched the child with a chuckle. "Sounds like an excuse for a nap. I'm in. Shall we?" He wrapped his free arm around Gaia and then popped them into a room with his boy, who slept soundly until they arrived.

Junior woke, rubbing his eyes. He lifted his arms. "Da."

Lucifer reached for his son, and Jujube yelled, "My Da. Me. Me."

That didn't please Gaia. "Mama has you." Indeed, she had lifted the girl from Lucifer's arms during their transition.

"Da. Me," Jujube insisted.

Whereas the boy hugged Lucifer and offered a smug, "My daddy."

Which led to a sibling scream fest that put Jujube in his arms and sent Gaia fleeing.

How long could he keep thwarting her?

10

THE MINUTES after Julio left were the most terrifying of Helen's life. She'd not realized how safe she'd felt in his presence. How inconspicuous under the cover of his cloak.

With him gone, the Earthly plane crashed all her senses. She could barely handle all the color smeared everywhere. For an angel used to the muted pastels of heaven, the brightness and disharmony proved jarring. An overload to her senses rendered worse by the noise. Loud machines rumbled along on wheels. Everything hummed with electricity. The noise was almost enough to make her slap her hands over her ears, only she realized no one else was reacting. No one cared.

The people in the streets walked along as if those flashing bright signs weren't stabbing their eyes. Or the cars going by weren't belching smoke. They ignored those things but kept turning to eye her.

She glanced down at her voluminous night robe and her slippers. She needed to blend in. And quickly.

However, everywhere she turned, she was struck with the alien-ness of everything. Where should she go? Why hadn't she accepted Julio's offer of help? Because that would be like accepting the devil's aid, and she knew that was a sin. She couldn't exactly claim innocence if she did the dark lord's bidding.

Scared and unsure of what to do next, Helen began to walk aimlessly, hugging herself as she left the busy streets for quieter ones with deep pockets of shadow. A few cars drove by, their bright lights blinding in the dark.

One slowed, and a window rolled down. "Hey, honey, you look lost. You want a ride?"

The idea of not walking filled Helen with intense relief. Her feet hurt. How kind of the man to offer.

Helen reached for the car door, only to have someone insert herself, literally pushing Helen out of the way. A very feminine voice purred, "Not tonight, sugar. She's not ready."

Before Helen could ask, "Not ready for what?", the man snapped, "Mind your business, cunt. If the chick wants to make twenty bucks sucking my dick, then—"

The woman suddenly shoved her head through the open car window and said very softly but firmly, "I said no. And no means no, fuckwad. Now go because if I see you again, I will separate you from the two-inch joke in your pants."

"Yes, ma'am." The car tires screamed something awful as he drove away, and the woman turned around.

She was pretty with blonde hair tied back and wearing an outfit of pink that included loose pants, a tucked-in blouse, and a fluffy jacket. She offered a smile to Helen. "Sorry about that. Some people are just so rude. I'm Bambi." She held out a hand.

Eyeing it, Helen wondered what to do with it and replied, "I'm Helen."

"Nice to meet you, Helen, and in the nick of time apparently. Good thing I found you. My Father wasn't kidding when he said you needed a crash course on living on Earth."

"Your Father?" Her eyes widened as she clued in. "You're Lucifer's daughter!"

"Yes, I am. The less famous one. The one you've probably heard of is Muriel, my younger sister."

"Your sister is the world's biggest whore?" Which she understood was someone who indulged in much fornication outside of marriage.

Bambi's lips quirked. "Actually, that's me. Multiverse winner many years in a row."

"Isn't being a whore a bad thing?"

The beautiful woman flipped her hair. "Not everyone is repressed about their sexuality. Do you even know what sex is, little cherub?"

"I'm not a cherub." That was a name used for babies.

"You're innocent like one. But don't worry, we'll fix that."

"How?"

"By teaching you what you need to know to survive in this world."

"Can I survive?" She'd begun to wonder.

"Anyone can. It's just a matter of learning and preparing."

"I don't know if I have enough time. The devil claims there is a warrant for my arrest." How could anyone believe those lies!

"And? So what if there's a price on your head. I've got a few. As does my sister, her four husbands, even my sweet little niece."

That sounded like a few too many husbands. "Why do people want to kill you? How have you sinned?" Helen asked.

"I'm a whore, remember? My sister is, too, and a polygamist. Which personally, to me, is more like a lucky girl. I used to think I'd be the one to settle down with a football team, and yet there is only one man who makes my heart beat faster."

"That's a good thing?" Helen asked, because a quickening heart could mean a health issue. While rare, angels did still have some mishaps.

"Love should make your heart pitter patter, your panties wet, and make you feel as if you're dying every minute you spend apart."

"That doesn't sound pleasant."

"Don't knock it until you try it."

"I am not sinning."

"You say that now, but..." Bambi winked. "Just you wait. Once you meet the one, it's all over."

For some reason she thought of Julio and his dark gaze.

"You look like you could use a drink. What do you say we go back to my place?"

Go somewhere with the devil's progeny? Helen wanted to say no; however, here was someone who could give her answers. Could it be as simple as asking? "Do you know how angel babies are made?"

Bambi coughed. "Yeah, but let's not discuss that on the street." Bambi swirled her hand, and a dark space cut the air in front of them. "Shortcut to my condo. Follow me."

Helen only hesitated a second. She didn't really want to be alone.

She exited the strange portal to find herself in front of a door in a hall lit by wall sconces.

"Welcome to my home." Bambi opened the portal.

Upon entering, Helen noticed it was probably a thousand times the size of her room in Heaven and luxurious to the point it surely constituted a sin. Carpet underfoot, plush and squishy. Furniture that had cushions to cradle the body.

"What is that?" she asked, pointing to the long fabric-covered thing that reminded her of a partially enclosed bed.

"A couch. It's for sitting."

"Really?"

"Try it."

Helen sank onto it and sighed. "This is very comfortable." Surely this kind of luxury was against the rules.

"You've never sat on a couch?"

Helen shook her head and ran her hand over the cushions. "I've only ever seen a fabric-covered chair in the Archnanny's office." But that was for Rafaella, not the nannies. Usually when called in front of the Archnanny, it was for rebuke and they weren't offered comfort.

"If you think that's fancy, wait until you see your bedroom."

"You have more than one room in your home?" This large space had more space?

"Yes. Four bedrooms and a few bathrooms as well so we don't have to share."

"What's a bathroom?" While she did have some basic knowledge, like the fact humans used cars instead of horse-drawn carriages, she didn't know how they lived.

"Oh boy, this is going to be interesting. Because now that you're here on Earth, things will be different for you."

"It's not what I expected at all. It's nothing like Heaven."

"What is Heaven like?" Bambi asked.

"It's the most perfect place."

"Why?"

What an odd question. "Everyone knows it is."

"And again, why? What makes it so desirable?" Bambi insisted, and Helen struggled to remember what she'd learned in class.

"It's not Hell for one. It's always sunny. Never rains. Never snows. Never gets too cold or hot. Everyone has a place to live. A job to do. We always have a meal that is balanced to our needs. Prayer. And the love of our Father, who art our shepherd in Heaven."

"Sounds more like you're mindless peons for the dictator known as Elyon."

Helen's jaw dropped. "What? That's not what I said."

"Then maybe you should examine your words. Do you get to do what you want? Did you have a say in your job? Your life?"

"We are assigned our role. Everyone does their part. As our Father—who is wise in Heaven—says, 'we are all in this together.'"

Bambi snorted. "Fuck me, I wondered where that expression came from. Should have known. And no, you angels are not all in it together. You're chattel."

"You work for your Father," Helen pointed out.

"I do, but I can also tell him to go screw a hairy hog if I don't want to do something. I run the risk of being smote, but dear Daddy doesn't like it when we're obedient all the time."

"Obedience is next to our Father, who is the most hallowed of his name."

Bambi blinked. "What the fuck? Do you say something dumb like that every time you say Father?"

"It's not dumb," Helen defended. "We honor him."

"Really?" Bambi's expression turned sly. "Rumor has it he's being held prisoner by Charlie. How's that being honorable?"

"Our Father, who is on a sabbatical, is recovering."

"From launching a war that he lost before it even started."

"Was there really a battle?" In the nursery, items of news were few and far between. No corrupting the nannies after all.

"More like Elyon crashed my niece's birthday party and a bunch of cake and fists were tossed. Muriel had a tantrum because they ruined Lucinda's day, my daddy, who is rancid after eating spicy foods, had to be restrained, especially after your Father, who is an idiot in Heaven, talked smack about Gaia."

"Who is Gaia?"

"Mother Earth."

"Earth is her child?" That made no sense.

"I see we'll need to start from the beginning."

"Do you mean when my Father, may he forever be blessed, created the world?"

"It starts before that actually, with a big bang."

And Helen got a second version of creation, a story so incredible she wouldn't believe it.

Couldn't.

Because if she did, then it meant Heaven, and all its rules, was a lie.

11

I CAN'T BELIEVE they left me in charge.

The commander had taken off and left Julio responsible for the company. Piece of upside-down pineapple cake. All he had to do was ensure everybody showed up and did their jobs.

However, no one left instructions on what to do when Helen—the virgin! —walked in and caught him with his feet up on the desk. Wearing white slacks, a white blouse, with white shoes and an off-white blazer, she entered, chewing her lower lip.

"You're back. How can I help you?"

She clasped her hands in front of her and kept her eyes downcast. He almost had to strain to hear her soft, "I need to find out how angel babies are made."

"Sure. Shall we have the demonstration on the desk or in a bed?"

Her lips pursed. "I was not asking for fornication."

"Um, a little confused, because how do you think babies are made?"

"Sex might make human babies, but angels are different."

"Says who?"

"Me."

"And who else?"

"Everyone in Heaven."

"It's a lie."

"Really? Then explain why there are no pregnant angels in Heaven." She had a ready argument.

He almost felt bad for her, knowing what he did. "That's because Elyon's got the females on birth control."

"He does not! You're as bad as Bambi," she exclaimed.

"You've spoken with Bambi?"

"She spent the last few days teaching me about your world and trying to convince me that Heaven is a lie."

And not succeeding, apparently, since Curls was standing in front of him with her cheeks pink.

"Hate to break it to you, but Heaven is all kinds of false." He took his feet off the desk and leaned forward. "Do you know why there are no pregnant angels in Heaven? It's because Elyon rendered the females sterile."

"Our Father, who—" Helen halted and snapped, "He wouldn't do that. Our babies are created by our Father, who is the creator in Heaven, and delivered by storks not...between the...from the..." She turned red as she gestured and stammered.

"Is this your way of saying you don't think angel babies are shoved out vaginas?"

Her cheeks were so hot he might have been able to fry bacon on them. "I'm not that naïve. A baby would never fit out of there."

"I'll admit, it's shocking, but true. Let me know if you'd like to see a live birth. I'm sure we can find someone who won't mind an audience." Helen appeared speechless, and he grinned. "Keep your mouth open like that and—" He almost said something dirty about having the perfect thing for it but amended it to, "you'll catch flies."

It snapped shut before she muttered, "You are so annoying. I should have stuck with Bambi as a teacher."

"Please do. I'm sure it won't be long before she's teaching you how to wear fewer clothes. Maybe show off your tits. Teach you how to smile." He added a leer to his suggestions, knowing they were misogynistic as fuck, but her huffing and puffing embarrassment amused. Not to mention, she should learn to handle dirty talk with someone safe before she met a prick who knocked her off balance.

Chin tilted, she sassed, "I will not be removing my clothes. Nudity leads to sin."

"Yes, it does." He winked. "Babies, too."

"According to the devil's helpers."

"Really? Let me ask you, where do you think baby angels come from? Because the stork obviously gets them from somewhere."

Her shoulders rolled. "I don't know. Perhaps they are born of a seed in the bole of a magical tree."

He snorted. "Now you're pushing it and being

overly stubborn. Angels are born the same way as humans."

"And how is that possible? After all, didn't you say angels are sterile?" She threw back his claim, not knowing all the facts.

"Females are, but male angels aren't. Heaven relies on cross breeding, Curls. Apparently, angels and humans are compatible when it comes to making babies. Says so right here in my book."

He reached into the desk and pulled out a massive tome that showed its age with the worn leather, previously worn by an animal that probably never walked the Earth. The office used it to ensure proper compatibility when setting up the visiting demons with possible baby mamas and dadas.

"What is that?" she asked, nearing in fascination.

"The Hellacious Book of Demonic Beasts."

She recoiled.

"Ignore the grand title. It's an encyclopedia of beings. It's got entries on every single living creature, including angels."

"Someone wrote about us?" She couldn't hide her curious note.

"Curls, there are hundreds, thousands of stories about angels, most of them garbage, I should add. But this...this is what we call non-fiction. Researched and peer reviewed." He slapped his hand on the cover, repeating the words he'd memorized when he'd visited Chad in archives, looking for information on angels.

He flipped open the book, which wasn't exactly

alphabetical, given it was constantly being added to. At least this version had a magical auto update and an index.

"Angels. Page three thousand and forty-three." He opened the book wide at random and, as per the magic, landed on the right page. He scrolled to the correct section and zoomed it. "Shall I read it?"

"No. I can do that myself."

It wasn't a very long passage. It stated male angels could procreate, and with humans only. Acceptable progeny would be delivered to Heaven. Those lacking wings remained on Earth. Along with the info, there was also a warning. Absolutely no fornication with any denizens of Hell. Punishable by death. Permanent death, as in don't stop at Hell or linger in Limbo. Right into the pit of perdition for recycling.

Harsh.

She recoiled. "That can't be true."

"It's right there in print."

She flattened her lips. "And I'm saying it's impossible. What your book claims would require thousands of angels and our Father, who art silent in Heaven, being complicit."

"Yup. It's a massive conspiracy. But you can change that."

"Me?"

"What if you were to bring the truth to Heaven?"

She bit her lip. "Who would listen? I am still struggling to believe."

"How about if I could show you proof?"

"What kind of proof?" she asked.

The kind that would start the revolution the devil hoped for.

12

JULIO OFFERED to show her proof that angels consorted with humans to make babies. Surely it was a lie. A mistake.

Although she no longer doubted that some angels sinned and fornicated. She'd seen Michelina disobeying and had been on Earth long enough to realize sex was a popular thing to do.

But his claim about cherubs being made the same way as animals?

Devastating if true because it would mean yet another lie in a chain of them. Such as the one claiming Earth was a dirty, sinful place and Heaven the good. For all that she'd had to learn and overcome culture wise, the last few days had been the most interesting of her life.

The sights. The sounds. The people.

She'd met more than a few because Bambi insisted on dragging her around when she showed up at random times during the day. She'd ordered Helen to stop watching television—the most annoying demand coming right in the middle of a show called *Witcher* where a fellow with white hair showed off his impressive sword skills. Helen couldn't have said why she found it riveting, yet there was something about the strong and dexterous man that drew her eye.

She'd looked away when the violence and carnal stuff happened on the screen. At least she did the first day. By the second, she had learned to use the ten-seconds back button, rewinding the things that fascinated or demanded more study.

It appeared humanity didn't just indulge in fornication; they reveled in it. Enjoyed sex. Watching it on screen left her feeling...odd. Tingly. Ashamed. It also had her thinking of Julio and feeling even more tingly.

What did it mean? She didn't dare ask even as Bambi seemed determined to teach.

Bambi said she couldn't learn everything by staying inside watching television. She made Helen wear pants —shocking!—and brought her into the world to explore. She introduced Helen to a chip truck, a vendor on the street who, for the tap of card, would provide flavorful sustenance. A bacon poutine, Bambi called it.

One bite and Helen inhaled the rest. She'd never imagined food could taste so incredible. And she didn't see the sin in it. No one got hurt. On the contrary, everyone was pleased by the transaction.

Poutine was only the start of the flavors she tested. In a cold box, called a fridge, there were jars and containers of food with tastes so varied she couldn't stop trying them and ended up on the floor, stomach distended, groaning. Her gluttony was punished by her hugging something cold and hard. Bambi blasphemed and called it the porcelain god.

Whatever it was, she donated copious amounts of puke to it. But worse was what came out of her bottom.

It turned out on Earth it wasn't just the animals who defecated.

As she lay groaning in bed, vowing to never eat again, she wished she'd never left heaven.

By the time she woke the next morning, she felt better, especially once she looked outside. No blue skies today. Water fell instead.

Rain.

Helen stood on the balcony, head tilted back, feeling it hit her skin in cold droplets. A day without sunshine, how refreshing. It made her curious about snow and storms and so much more.

"Are you done getting wet?" Bambi had hollered from inside. "Because I've got to leave, but before I do, I want to show you how to use the internet."

She taught Helen the basics of a mighty machine called the internet. It was so easy to get information. All Helen had to do was say, "Okay bitch-tits, find me —" fill in the blank. A little black box by the television would then reply and show the result on the screen. The thing called internet acted like a giant repository of information, smart enough to pull up anything Helen asked—which turned out to be a copious amount about angels.

It placed images of angels with big fluffy wings, robes, and haloes on the television for her to ogle.

"How is this possible?" she muttered. Humans weren't supposed to see angels. Only others of her kind should be able to see her wings, although it seemed those from Hell could see them, too.

Yet the pictures revealed humanity knew about angels, proved they interacted. More research showed there were enough stories to muddle any truth.

She discovered books about forbidden romances between angels and humans. Angels and demons. Movies featuring angels. Television shows.

How to separate truth from lie?

Currently, she relied on the devil's daughter to feed her information. However, Helen had more questions and wondered if the answers would change if she talked to someone else. Hence why she ended up making her way to the offices of Grim Dating to speak with the reaper who'd been on her mind since the moment they met. A man who said he could show her proof that Heaven was a lie.

Julio snapped his fingers. "Curls, I asked you a question. Do you want me to show you where babies come from or not?"

She did and didn't, which was why she admitted, "Is it odd that I do and don't?"

"I'd say that's a normal reaction to having your perception of the world turned upside down. Would it help if I said I'll be beside you the whole time?"

Actually, it did help. "What kind of proof do you have?"

"Come with me to find out." He rose and reminded her of his height. As he moved, she caught glimpses of his cloak, a living black fog that undulated at his back.

Exiting the building that she'd travelled to via something called a taxi, he insisted on driving. It meant being in close proximity with him in his truck, the kind that had a box in the back to carry things. The enclosed cab meant his scent was everywhere, as was his cloak, swirling and teasing around her.

She slapped at it. "Would you stop that?"

"Sorry. It likes you."

The inanity of the comment had her snorting. "A cloak doesn't feel."

"A reaper one does. It's a part of me and reacts to my environment and my emotions. I imagine your wings are the same."

Her nose wrinkled. "My wings are not satanic magic."

"Never said they were. I referenced the fact they're a part of you and yet, at the same time, can act independently if needed."

As if speaking woke them, she felt her wings shivering, invisible to humans on this plane. Like his cloak.

She cocked her head. "Can you manifest your garment for humans?"

"Yes, but I rarely bother."

"How is it that I can see it?"

He shrugged. "No idea, but I guess it has to do with the fact I can spot an angel even if their wings are tucked away."

"Have you met many angels?"

"A few. Goading Michael is one of my favorite things."

"*The* Michael?"

"If you mean the douchebag with blond hair and seriously annoying attitude, then yes."

At his lack of deference, she coughed. "He's one of the highest placed angels in Heaven." Everyone knew his name, and his rages. Michael came through the nursery once, ranting about the empty cribs, wanting to know why there weren't more babies. The Arch-nanny had followed at his heels and muttered something about contraception, which made no sense at the time.

But now... Her mind shied away from it. Not ready. She focused on Julio instead.

"Michael is a pompous ass, and it gives me immense pleasure to get him spitting mad," he said.

"And he hasn't punished you?" Michael was their greatest enforcer.

"I keep hoping he'll try." Julio winked at her.

"Shouldn't you be watching where you're driving?" She'd seen accidents on television. They didn't appear enjoyable.

"You're not dying in the next five minutes."

"How would you know?" she sassed.

"Reaper, remember? Imminent death always smells."

"Like what?"

"Depends on the person, but for me it's usually baking bread. Yeasty and yet delicious."

"Death smells good to you?" The idea seemed strange.

"Yup."

He turned onto a street and she asked, "Where are we going?"

"You asked for proof, and lucky for you, I happened upon the perfect thing. I'm going to introduce you to someone."

"Who?"

"You'll see in a minute." He parked his truck, and a moment later, they stood in front of a door painted a deep red.

At his brisk knock, a beautiful woman answered. Her hair was even curlier than Helen's. As she gazed at Helen, her face went through a series of expressions before settling on incredulous. "Okay, did someone put pot in the brownies again, or are you wearing a halo?"

"What? No." Helen put a hand to her head as she felt for it. If visible, it would be solid. Her fingers met nothing but air, meaning the woman in front of her must be like Julio, some kind of Hell minion who could see it, and yet she appeared quite human. Could there be others capable of seeing her true nature?

"Hey, Samantha. We spoke on the phone. I'm Julio with Grim Dating." He held out his hand.

"Oh, I'm surprised to see you here. I only submitted an application to your company on a lark. That logo with the cute little reaper..." Samantha rolled her shoulders and chuckled.

"And I'm so glad you did because your portfolio caught my eye. May we come in?"

"Of course." Samantha stepped aside and ushered them into the living room where he sat on the couch, Helen by his side. "Can I get you a drink? Coffee? Water?"

"We're fine. And I'll be sure to add gracious hostess to your profile." Julio leaned forward and smiled. "You're just the type of candidate we like. I'm convinced we'll be able to find your perfect match."

"I can't wait. I haven't dated in forever. It will be kind of nice to have the vetting process taken out of my hands. I figure you can't do any worse than I have." Samantha laughed despite the self-deprecating comment.

"Don't you worry. Grim Dating is all about making the right matches." Julio smiled at the other woman, and Helen got annoyed, even though she couldn't have explained why.

It soured her mood and words. "Why are we here? I thought you said you had proof to show me."

"I'm getting to it. Tell me, have you noticed anything different about Samantha?"

"She's very attractive for a human." It made her self-conscious.

Samantha snorted. "Wow. Complimented and insulted in one shot. I'm not human, sweetie."

"Then what are you?" Helen asked. She saw no sign of wings, or anything that set Samantha apart from other humans.

"Can't you smell it?"

Helen could only smell a jumbled mess that meant nothing to her. "I smell a great many things."

"I'm a shapeshifter. My other form is a wolf."

"You're an animal?" Helen's eyes widened.

"We're all animals, sweetie."

Helen shook her head. "No. I'm not." She glanced at Julio. "I don't understand why we're here."

"That makes two of us. Why are you really here? Because it's becoming obvious it's not only because of my application." Samantha arched a brow.

"I'm afraid my visit did have a secondary purpose. Helen is a new client of ours, currently under the misconception that angels can't make babies."

To which Samantha snorted. "You're fucking kidding me."

He shook his head. "Nope."

Samantha eyed Helen. "Where do you think angel babies come from?"

Why did Helen blush as she said, "The stork brings them."

Samantha couldn't stop laughing and all the while Helen got more and more annoyed. Finally, Samantha wiped at her wet eyes and said, "Holy fuck, that was funny."

"Except for the fact she truly believes it," Julio added.

"Now I see why you're here." Samantha then yelled, "Lector, get in here."

A small boy entered, sporting big shiny eyes, curly blond hair, a dimple in his cheek. A gorgeous child who ran to his mother, meaning Helen could see his back.

And the outline of his wings.

A roaring filled her ears. She couldn't blink, and her

eyes dried as she stared at the boy crawling into his mother's lap. A cherub. Here. On Earth.

How could this be?

"Where did you find him? Did you pick him in a cabbage patch?" she asked through wooden lips.

"I wish! Took me a full day of labor before I could push out his giant head. I thought my twat would never recover. He's my son. One hundred percent."

"And the Father?" Julio softly prodded.

"What do you think?" was Samantha's sarcastic reply. "His daddy was an angel."

Helen was frozen in place as it hit her. "Heaven lied." The Archangels, the teachers, everyone.

Samantha set the child down and eyed Helen. "Did they lie? Or did they just not tell you? Because Theodore, Lector's Father, was fully aware he could make babies. It's why he wore a rubber. Only it broke."

"And you're sure Theodore was an angel?" she asked to clarify.

Samantha nodded. "Wings, halo, and all. It's kind of why I slept with him."

"If you were sleeping, then how do you know he is the Father?"

"By sleeping, I mean we fucked. Twice. He called me a few days later, but I blew him off. He was only okay in the sack and boring out of it. When I found out I was pregnant, I tried to call, but his number was out of service. He doesn't know he's a Father, and I had no idea how to contact him."

"We don't have phones in Heaven. I think," Helen added musingly. "I wonder if it was just the nursery that lacked amenities." She glanced at Julio. "The night I went for a walk, I heard music. I saw people out and not seemingly worried about breaking rules. As if they didn't have to obey them." Her head dipped. "Why do they live differently than the nannies? Why are we punished if we don't obey every single rule? Why couldn't we have the same freedom as others?"

Julio had an answer. "Because there is no perfect system. Thinking, feeling people won't act the same. There are some who will always force their will, their view, on others."

"But why? How does it make sense to lie to us? They outlawed laughter," she huffed.

He winced. "Yeah, that's kind of brutal."

"If you don't like it, change it," Samantha suggested. "You know Heaven's secret. Reveal it. The more people, or in this case angels, who know the truth of how things really are, the more likely you are to change things."

"How can I tell anyone? I don't know how to get home."

Even as she said it, uncertainty filled her on whether she wanted to return. Especially as she glanced over at Lector, who'd climbed the table and leaped off it, the outline of his wings spreading, not taking shape in this reality but reacting nonetheless.

A cherub on Earth. Were there more like him?

"Does he shapeshift into a wolf as well?" Julio asked.

Samantha shook her head. "No, but he's young yet. Some don't trigger until their teen years. Others need a full moon."

The idea of the child changing shapes boggled the mind. But when the boy suddenly came close and grabbed her hand, his eyes peering into hers, she began to breathe quickly. He was living proof angels could make babies.

Male angels could, but she couldn't. Because someone decided she shouldn't.

God. Her lying Father in his prison. He'd done this to her.

That didn't sit well.

13

POOR HELEN. Julio had shattered her worldview by introducing her to a Nephilim. Hard to ignore visual evidence. But would Helen run with it? Start a revolution in Heaven?

Samantha had nudged her in that direction, but rather than fly into a rage and promise retribution, Helen grew quiet.

Quiet people could be frightening, as it could mean many things. Some mentally shut down, caving to pressure. Others plotted the kind of revenge that required meticulous detail—and didn't leave a body. The latter made prosecution more difficult. He'd learned that after one of his arrests.

Helen abruptly stood and said, "This has been most enlightening." And not entirely welcome judging by her expression.

Rather than rub Helen's face in the lies she'd been told, Samantha gave her a piece of advice. "You seem like a nice girl. Which is probably your problem. Nice girls follow all the rules, but those who break them don't care about hurting you. It's not a bad thing to look after yourself."

"Selfishness is a sin."

She spoke by rote, which was why Julio felt a need to say, "So is blindly following."

Helen's lips pursed. "Angels aren't supposed to fib."

"And I'd wager a good chunk of them don't." He shrugged. "But given they're half human, it's not hard to imagine there are a few that don't follow all the rules."

Samantha uttered a disparaging snort. "I'd say more than a few."

To that, Helen shook her head. "There are others like me who believed everything."

He wondered if she noted her use of the past tense.

"You should look up some failed forms of government when you get a chance," Samantha suggested. "The kind of society you're talking about is one that's failed many times, usually because they were conquered or their own people rose against them."

"You've given me much to ponder." Then more softly, "Thank you."

Julio quickly rose and extended his hand. "Yes, thank you, Samantha, for meeting with us. You seem like a fine candidate for Grim Dating, and I will personally oversee your match." A shapeshifter with a demon would create a fine minion for Lucifer.

With the good-byes spoken, Helen couldn't leave fast enough. She climbed into his truck and didn't say a word.

Definitely plotting someone's death. Hopefully not his. He'd hate to have to restrain her.

With her body under his.

Hmm. Maybe he should let her attack.

He headed for his office, having no idea where else to go. As they neared the building, he slowed, having spotted a shape dressed in white up ahead.

"What is it?" she asked, roused from her silent contemplation.

"I think I see one of your buddies from Heaven."

"Where?" She craned forward and grimaced. "I can't see their face."

"Might be your buddy with the sword." It would be brazen of him to come for her in plain sight. Julio had never reaped an angel, and yet, half human meant they had to have some kind of soul.

"I don't care who it is. I don't want to speak to them. Not yet. Can we go somewhere without people? I need to think. Ask questions." Her glance held trouble and angst.

It begged him for help, and he couldn't say no.

"We can go to my place. It's private. I also have stuff in the fridge if you're thirsty or hungry."

"Let's go." That was all she said before looking out her window. Despite saying she wanted to ask him things, she remained quiet.

He attempted to kick-start conversation. "So, I hear that chicken sandwich with no bread is coming back."

No reply.

Wait, were angels vegan? "Do you eat meat?"

"I do now." She wrung her hands. "I didn't realize

meat was a thing until Bambi fed me. I asked for the name of what I ate, and she told me it was chicken." Her head dipped. "It was delicious."

She sounded ashamed. As a carnivore, he heartily approved of her taste buds. "What kind of chicken did you try? My favorite is stuffed chicken. Smoked meat, cheese, and bacon on the inside, pan fried in seasoning and butter." Add some browned rice with freshly chopped chive for a side dish and he had a happy mouth and belly.

"I should be on my knees praying for forgiveness at having eaten flesh."

"But?"

"That sounds delicious," she admitted softly. "Maybe I am a sinner like the devil said because I want to taste everything."

"What did you eat in Heaven? Ambrosia of your god?" he asked, only semi-sarcastic.

"I wouldn't call it ambrosia. Twice a day we consumed a thick broth with all the nutrients we require."

He gagged. "That sounds gross."

She took offence. "It is not disgusting."

"Is it amazing?"

"It's necessary. I looked forward to the meals. But..." She chewed her lip. "Since being here, I've discovered so many flavors and textures. Hot and cold. Crunchy or soft. So many different reasons to like what's in my mouth."

"Name your favorite food so far." He'd rather chat about yummy treats and keep her engaged than remind her of what she'd discovered. It sucked he'd had to be the one to shatter her entire reality, but she deserved the truth.

She canted her head. "I am enjoying many things. Bananas are very good. Nice for gripping. and I like that I can just put it in my mouth and bite off as much as I can fit."

The more she spoke, the more his mind fell into the gutter. He changed the subject. "I have no bananas at my place"—if he ignored the one in his pants—"but I've got ice cream."

"Ooh. I love ice cream." She clapped her hands.

"What flavor?"

"All of them. Bambi took me to a place where they had numerous large buckets. We got a scoop from each of them."

By the time they arrived at his place, she'd waxed eloquent on three savory choices above all others. Butter pecan, cookie dough, and good old-fashioned chocolate.

His apartment was within an older building, a bit shabby around the edges, but she still stared around with avid interest then made a beeline for his couch. She sat on it and stroked the leather. "Very smooth and soft."

He didn't mention it was animal. "It's cold if you sit naked."

Her eyes widened, and her cheeks turned pink. "I'll remember to keep my clothes on then."

"Pity."

He knew she caught the implication by the way her

gaze dropped but her temperature rose. His cloak flicked out to touch her, and she turned to glance at him.

"Is it you making it touch me when I'm upset?"

He rolled his shoulders. "Yes and no. We are one and, at the same time, not. It is in tune to my emotions and reacts."

"It appears to be comforting me."

"Because it is."

"In Heaven, we don't comfort. Ever. We are stoic. We do not burden others with our emotions. There is no such thing as sorrow or fear. We must not get angry."

"You're implying angels can't feel. I think that's kind of an impossible rule, don't you?"

She paused for a moment before replying. "It is. A lot of the rules are difficult and make no sense."

"But you followed them."

"Mostly." She shrugged. "I got sent for contemplation more than once."

"That's what usually happens when you don't toe the line in a strict regime. And now you have even more questions."

"Yes."

"Do you want to talk about Lector?"

Her expression turned somber, and her hands knotted in her lap. "Not really."

"His existence answers your question about where babies come from."

"Is it proof, though? Perhaps he's part bird. His mother claims to be a wolf."

That caused him to utter a snort. "I saw you recognize the fact he's an angel baby."

"We call them cherubs."

"Whatever. He's an angel. Don't deny it."

She slumped. "He does appear to be one, and I would know. I was one of the nannies who helped care for them until they reached a certain stage of development."

She said it so clinically, he had to ask, "Did you like your job?"

A pensive mien overtook her features. "I don't know. At the time I did it because caring for them was my task. Did I like it?" Her frown intensified. "We never thought of it in those terms."

"What about your free time? What did you do for fun and relaxation?"

"In between prayers, I took care of myself."

"Surely you did more than that. What did you do for you that you enjoyed?"

She didn't answer.

His chest tightened. "Did you ever have fun?"

Her shoulders rolled. "Frivolity leads to sin."

"What the fuck kind of bullshit is that?" he exclaimed. "Seriously, Curls, you can't tell me you really believed you had to follow all that crap. I mean, what's the point of living if you can't be happy? I swear, hearing about Heaven makes me glad I earned a spot in Hell. It sounds horrible."

"It's not that..." She stopped talking and looked him dead in the eyes when she said, "It was all I ever knew."

"And now?"

She rolled her shoulders. "Now, I'm questioning everything."

He would help her with those questions and show her it wasn't the end of the world. But she might need some fortification. "Want a drink?"

"Yes."

He poured them both two fingers in a glass. She downed hers and choked.

"Your water burns," she gasped.

"It's whiskey. It's supposed to burn. Guess I should have asked." He wasn't used to someone who'd never drank. In his lifetime, pouring one was second nature.

"It feels hot." She put her hand to her chest.

"Yup." He poured them both another. "It'll spread, and you'll relax."

"Relax? I would like that." She downed the glass again, barely wincing this time. He poured a third shot, but she held on to it as she leaned back on his couch. She sighed. "I love couches. In the nursery we only had hard chairs and, in our rooms, a stone slab for a bed."

"Doesn't sound too heavenly. I thought you guys were supposed to have the best of the best."

"We are equal. Or so I thought. Those not in the nursery have different things than us. The Archnannies have larger rooms and more than a single gown." Her voice rose. "And I've heard say they don't have to scrub the halls or tend the paths outside."

"You can say it, Curls. It's not fair."

She struggled but managed to repeat, "It's not fair. We are supposed to all be the same."

"That kind of thinking is communism, Curls. Doesn't usually work as a system in the long term."

"It would if they let everyone have the same things."

"But some people like to have more than others."

"It's greedy."

"It's human."

The word saw her clamping her lips shut, angry at the reminder of her partial humanity.

"What are you feeling right now?" he prodded.

"I am..." She paused. "I am wanting you to stop talking."

"Because I'm pissing you off."

"You are annoying."

"Only because I'm right."

Her turn to make a noise. "You are taking pleasure in trying to turn me against Heaven. But my faith is solid. My Father, who is watching over me from Heaven, is probably testing me."

"You'd be wrong. But hey, you're allowed to make mistakes. Also a human thing." He couldn't help but dig.

For a second, her nostrils flared, and he expected her to explode. But she calmed and with a serene smile said, "Your home is much like Bambi's."

He snorted. "I highly doubt my apartment and hers are anywhere close to the same."

"You both have a big home. A couch. Table. Chair. A kitchen place." She swept a hand.

"Ah, you mean we both have stuff. So could you. On Earth, and even in Hell, anyone can own shit, but in most cases, you gotta work for it. In my case, to fill this place with useless crap, I have a job with Grim Dating. Get a job and you could own a bunch of useless shit too."

"A television is not useless."

He arched a brow. "Already addicted, eh?"

"It is the best thing I've ever encountered. Especially when accompanied by popcorn."

"With butter I hope."

"The slippery kind."

His mind fell in the gutter, and he recovered with, "You've experienced a lot in the three days since you arrived."

She nodded. "It's been very enlightening."

"In what respect?"

"Earth and humanity are much more complex and evolved than I'd been led to believe."

"Have you never spoken to a human soul?"

"I've never met one. Keep in mind, I worked inside the nursery. I saw only other nannies, guards, and the cherubs."

"Sounds like prison."

"We don't have prisons, as we don't commit crimes."

"So how do they punish those who break the rules?" he asked, curious. Because surely it happened.

"Transgressions can result in supplementary chores and prayers or time in solitary contemplation."

"Ouch. That sucks."

"It's all I ever knew. What is Hell like? We're told fire and brimstone and agony."

"Well, it is. For some. But most people have only committed minor sins, meaning their lives in Hell aren't being tortured day in and out. In Hell, only the truly depraved souls suffer hard. Everyone else just kind of ekes out an existence."

"Murdering. Torturing. Stealing."

He snorted. "Well, yeah, it is Hell after all. But because there is free choice, there are those who work. We are allowed to laugh and even love."

"So some sinners do repent and live righteously after their descent."

That made him laugh. "Oh, Hell no. On the contrary, being in the rings means a slackening of the morals that kept them in check while alive."

"It must be absolute chaos and anarchy then."

"Not exactly because we have some rules. Basic ones. For example, if you're going to steal, you can only steal from someone more fortunate than yourself."

"Thieves can only steal from the rich?"

"Only the richer."

"How does that act as a determent?"

"Because as a thief advances through their career, their fortune will grow, and their choice in targets will narrow and become better protected. They will become a possible target themselves. Not to mention, Hell allows for retaliation. Attack me and I can attack you. It's a type of check and balance system." Look at him with his fancy jargon. He'd been reading up on the laws of Hell, a reminder that when he'd lived, before he'd turned to dirty tricks, he was going to be a lawyer.

"Stealing isn't allowed in Heaven," was Helen's observation.

"You're telling me it never happens? How can you be sure? Did you have anything to steal?"

Her mouth worked before she shook her head, her thick curls bouncing.

"In other words, you don't really know. What about murder? And before you say no, remember how I found you in that alley." A minute later and he'd have been too late.

"I haven't forgotten." Her head ducked.

"Speaking of which, has there been any attempt to kill you since then?"

"No! But Bambi did tell me to lie low and not go out without her. Although I am not sure how lying down is supposed to help."

"It's an expression meaning stay out of sight, and you did the opposite of that coming to my office"

She shrugged. "I don't want to hide. Not when I still need answers."

"What questions do you have left?"

Once more, she hesitated before answering. "It's not one you can answer."

"Try me."

"If it is true angels make babies with humans, then how did the storks miss Lector?"

"I imagine the fact his father never knew about him played a part."

She couldn't help a dubious, "Maybe he just looks like a cherub."

"We both know that kid is half angel. I think the more important question is, have angels been stealing babies this entire time?"

"It's not stealing. They're angels."

"They're also half human, and they're being taken from their mothers."

Her mouth rounded. "Humans are emotional beings who care for their progeny."

"And taking a child away is devastating because humans love their children. Why do you think Samantha never tried too hard to find Theodore and tell him about his kid?"

"She wanted to make sure the storks wouldn't come for him." She glanced at her hands in her lap for a moment before saying softly, "The more I discover, the more I question if I want to return."

"The fact you're asking might help with that reply," was his contribution.

"Heaven is where angels belong."

"Is it? What about your human half? Ever wonder if your mother would have given you a better life?"

She blinked. "I hadn't until now. Thanks." Said so grumpily he knew it was sarcastic.

"It never occurred to you, did it?"

"The concept of motherhood is one I only learned of today. Give me a moment to process it."

"Would you rather I shut up?"

"No." Her lips quirked. "However, if I'm going to have my entire belief system shattered, then I could do with some of that food you promised."

She looked so hopeful he laughed. It was as they worked in the kitchen—him getting out some leftovers for heating and her exploring everything—that they ended up toe to toe, face to face.

She paused. "Sorry. I am in your way."

"Don't be. You're curious." She'd been peeking in his cupboards, avid interest in everything, even texture as she ran her fingertips over items.

"I've only seen Bambi's condo, and yours is different."

"You mean smaller, I imagine." He grinned. "Easier to keep clean."

"I like your place better."

"Because my décor isn't about look but comfort. Just like my food is about filling that craving for carbs. Prepare to be wowed." He fed her leftover lemon chicken, dipped in sauce. They shared a box of reheated fried rice. She gnawed on riblets and groaned. Licked her fingers.

It enthralled him to the point she noticed his gaze and said, "Why do you stare at me?"

"Because you're beautiful." The words spilled, and he could have dropped in shock.

"Everyone is beautiful," she said, staring at him. Her chair was close enough it wouldn't take much to lean in.

"It's not everyone I want to kiss."

"Kiss." Her glance went to his lips. "It's forbidden. Especially between our kind."

"I know." And that only made it hotter.

She cocked her head. "If I kiss you, I will never make it back to Heaven."

He couldn't help a cocky grin. "Don't be so sure of that." He winked.

She sucked in a breath and then decided for them.

She pressed her mouth to his.

That was it. She held it there as his eyes crinkled. She stared at him then mumbled, "Am I doing it wrong?"

"Try moving your mouth like this." He then proceeded to kiss her, showed her how to slide sensually. To nibble. Taste. He kissed her until she got the hang of it and kissed him right back.

She clung to him, and it seemed only natural for her to end up in his lap, squirming against his erection. Not that she understood what her actions did to him.

She wore pants, but that didn't stop him from skimming his hand up her thigh and cupping her. She uttered a sound, and her hips jerked.

He kept kissing her and turned her so she straddled him, better able to control the hard pressure and grind he placed against her, gauging his effects by her gasps and how far her head fell back. She let herself roll against him, the friction enough to make her tighten and cry out.

He held her trembling body, wanting to do more, giving her a chance to recover.

She sounded amazed as she said, "What was that?"

"Your first orgasm." Hell yeah, he swelled with pride.

"That was..." She couldn't speak, but she did squirm. His turn to groan.

"Am I hurting you?" she asked.

"Yes, but in a good way." He drew her in for another kiss and was ready for round two when they were interrupted by the devil.

14

THE DARK LORD really didn't have time to be going to the mortal plane to save a stupid reaper who'd broken a cardinal rule. However, Julio and Helen still had a role to play, so despite the loss of half of his eighth ring overnight, and a riot in the sixth as it got overrun by the encroaching refugees from seven and what remained of eight, he made the time to help a minion in need.

And was the fucker grateful?

"Get the fuck out!" Julio bellowed, while the angel squeaked and buried her face against his chest.

"Are you sure you want me to do that? Because you're about to have company. Angels to be exact. Here to arrest Helen. Hi, Helen," Lucifer added just to hear her squeak again.

"What the fuck are you talking about?" Julio gently set her aside and stood, a bristling alpha male.

Lucifer had a preference for tough people as

reapers. They better handled the sobbing when they encountered a reluctant soul.

"You were ratted out, and now they're coming for the girl." No need to mention the fact he'd called in the tip himself. He needed to create a sense of urgency.

"We won't answer," Julio growled.

"As if they won't break in." The devil couldn't help but play his own advocate. "Did I mention they have permission to use force to apprehend the disgraced Helen? Rumor is they'd prefer she not return alive."

"How many?" Julio shook his head. "Doesn't matter. We should go."

"Go where?" Helen asked.

That was Lucifer's cue. "If you go anywhere on Earth, they'll just follow. Chase poor Helen here until, during a struggle as she resists capture, she is 'accidentally' killed, her spirit sent to the great beyond." Lucifer flung a hand, and sparkles erupted for effect. No one admired his excellent theatrics. Nope. Julio and Helen only had eyes for themselves.

Selfish fuckers.

Julio's cloak wrapped around Helen protectively. "Let's go somewhere."

"You still haven't said where," she reminded.

"I'd get going if I were you, before they have the place completely shut down." Lucifer waited.

Julio tried to do his thing. "Why can't I open a portal?"

"Because they're jamming your signal." Lucifer shrugged. "Guess you waited too long."

"Fucking great. Now what are we supposed to do? Jump out the window?" Julio snapped.

"I can fly us to safety," Helen offered.

"I doubt you'll get far. They have someone stationed on the roof." Lucifer couldn't stand the anticipation as they slowly came to the realization they were fucked.

"Then we'll use the emergency stairs," Julio suggested.

"Too late. Tick. Tock. Time is almost up." Lucifer held up a massive pocket watch on a chain of tiny skulls.

Julio's jaw clenched as he muttered, "Could you help us rather than taunt?"

"Help? I'm the devil. I don't just do things for nothing."

"How about if I owe you a favor?" Julio offered.

"Now you're talking. But I want a favor from her, too." Lucifer pointed.

"I won't—" The cloak slapped over her mouth as Julio answered for her, "Helen agrees."

Lucifer heaved a long sigh. "A Dark Lord's work is never done. Lucky for you, thwarting Heaven is my jam. Here's what we need to do." He told them his brilliant plan. They both said no.

A knock came at the door. along with a bellowed, "By order of Charlie, Elyon's only true and recognized son, open this door and hand over the rebel known as Helen."

The next time Lucifer posed his question, "Who wants to get married?" they both said, "I do."

15

MARRIED. A concept Helen had only ever read about. Because angels didn't do that. They didn't marry or have friendships. Angels didn't do so many things.

Angels most certainly never let the devil convince them to let him preside over a ceremony that bound her to Julio, making him her husband. As his wife, she became a de facto citizen of Hell.

She'd have laughed if she could have overcome her shock.

"Congratulations, you may kiss the bride," the devil said with a wink.

Julio might have been gruff when he said, "I do," but his kiss was soft.

The pounding on the door was hard.

"Good luck, newlyweds," the devil interrupted. "Gotta go. Can't be seen on Earth meddling."

Lucifer left as the door was kicked open and angels spilled in, led by one she recognized. The male angel who'd started this fiasco.

The angel pointed with his sword. "Surrender."

Julio shifted until Helen was shielded by his body, the edge of his cloak whispering over her. "She's not going anywhere with you, asshole."

"Stand aside, reaper. This is Heaven's business. We have a warrant for her arrest."

Julio shook his head. "Guess again. You and your band of feathery sycophants have no authority over a denizen of Hell."

"She's not been judged fallen. Not yet," the angel snapped. "Until she is, move aside, or I will—"

"What, fathead? What do you think you'll do, exactly?" Julio's cloak had turned into a tumultuous, roiling storm of shadow. He loomed, giving the impression of massive size.

The angel sneered. "You would defy Heaven's emissary?" The guy lifted his hand and curled his fingers. "Cut the reaper down and take the woman."

"Touch my wife and you'll die." Julio uttered the statement as a solemn promise

"She married you?" Disbelief followed by disdain. "You lie."

"I assure you, we are married."

She still couldn't believe it. Maybe if they'd had time for another kiss...

"Doesn't matter if you're married. She is under arrest."

"Actually, Theodore, it does matter." A woman suddenly appeared in a fog of dark blue that settled into a business suit. She wore a severe expression as she faced down the angel. "Hello, I'm Kourtney, Grim

Dating's legal counsel, here to explain why you cannot lay a hand on the new Mrs. Julio Reaper. You are hereby being reminded that Mrs. Reaper, as a result of her binding marriage to Julio Reaper, is now a citizen of Hell with all the rights and protections afforded that stature."

"So what if she married a reaper?" Theodore sneered. "You do realize it's just more proof she deserves arrest and punishment. The rules are clear. Angels may not consort with minions of Hell."

"A fallen angel can," Kourtney pointed out.

"Only she never stood trial and was never cast out," Theodore argued. "She broke our laws before the marriage. She will be tried for her crimes. It could be that instead of being cast down she is allowed to do penance."

Kourtney didn't back down. "You want her, then you'll have to file an extradition request."

"Or I can just take her now," Theodore threatened, taking a step forward.

Kourtney shook her head. "You really don't want to do that. There are rules you have to follow. Part of the treaty between Heaven and Hell signed after the hundred-year war. It says you can't take a citizen of Hell without going through the proper channels."

Theodore bristled with rage and raised his sword. "I don't listen to demons."

"Oh, you really don't want to do that," Julio admonished.

From nowhere a shadowy shape appeared and

spread at Kourtney's back. From it a voice boomed, "You would threaten my woman?"

Theodore glared at the newly arrived reaper. "This is Heaven's business."

"You don't want to fuck with me."

The reaper loomed, and Kourtney turned a smile on the spreading shadow and said, "Thanks, but I got this, Dwayne."

"Just making sure he realizes he can't threaten you."

Dwayne settled down, and Kourtney turned back to Theodore just as he said, "No one will be harmed if you stand aside."

"You want Helen, then you will abide by the contract. Any move on your part to take her by force will constitute a violation, and I will file a formal complaint."

"We should report this to Michael and see what he wants to do," said an angel at Theodore's back.

"I am not leaving without her." Theodore just wouldn't give up.

It was then Helen got brave and stepped forward. "If you're so worried about the rules, then why don't we talk about the fact you've been breaking them. I saw you fornicating with a nanny in Heaven."

Theodore's jaw tightened. "Stop with the lies."

"Lies?" she huffed. "I'm not the one who has a problem with the truth. I know you're a sinner. I've seen your son here on Earth. I know that Heaven is the one who has been lying. Our Father is not our Father in Heaven. We are made on Earth. We are half human."

At her words, the angels shifted, and Theodore's face darkened. "Blasphemy."

"It's the truth. And you want me so you can silence me before I tell anyone," she accused.

As Theodore's companions shifted away from him, he snarled, "This isn't over. I'll be back." A definite threat, and yet he and his squad left the apartment without arresting her, which she considered a victory.

Kourtney appeared somber. "He'll return, and soon, with Heaven's lawyer in tow. I recommend you be gone before then."

"Why? I thought they couldn't arrest me because we are married." She glanced at Julio, who appeared just as confused.

Kourtney's lips flattened. "Yes and no. The problem is there is a very hard rule about angels getting married to reapers. Actually, according to the quick search I did on angelic laws, your kind can't get married to anyone. Add in the non-association-with-Hell rule and we could be arguing this case in the neutral courts for a long time."

"I thought you said I was fallen?" An idea that didn't frighten her like it once did. Not after all she'd seen.

"Not technically. Theodore is correct in that you have to stand trial and be formally cast down."

"But I sinned."

Kourtney shrugged. "I don't make the laws, just argue for or against them."

"What are we supposed to do?" Julio asked. "I won't let them take her." Did he even notice how his cloak had reached out to wrap around her, keeping her warm when inside she felt chilled?

"Theodore isn't an angel who will accept defeat. Look at the lengths he's already gone to cover his misdeeds."

"What do you suggest then? If he won't stop chasing me, then does that mean I should turn myself in?" Helen didn't want to, and yet it seemed she didn't have a choice.

"I wouldn't." Kourtney shrugged, a roiling cloud of blue that merged with the black cloak still looming at her back. "Seems to me that'd ensure a certain death. The best thing I can suggest is to go somewhere Theodore can't reach you. Somewhere to give you breathing room while we try to clear your name."

"Is there such a place on Earth?" Julio asked.

Kourtney shook her head, but Dwayne had a suggestion. "There's only one place you can go where angels won't follow."

Hell.

16

JULIO DIDN'T NEED to look at Helen to know she'd be against the idea.

"I am not going to Hell," she muttered obstinately.

"Then I guess you're going to Heaven," he retorted. "And not the nice way."

Kourtney and Dwayne wisely took their leave.

"I haven't sinned." At Julio's arched brow, Helen amended her statement. "Much."

"It would only be temporarily while we deal with your angel problem."

"It wouldn't be a problem if people realized Theodore was a liar!" she yelled, finally indulging in her human half's emotions.

"And hopefully soon we'll be able to reveal just how crooked he is, but in the meantime, unless you want to be arrested and officially cast down, you don't have a choice." He didn't point out the fact that her becoming fallen was just a matter of time whether she appeared in Heaven to defend herself or not. She'd consorted with the devil, married a reaper, and made out with him on a kitchen chair. Plus, she'd eaten meat. When would she realize there was no going back?

A better question being, why would she want to?

Her shoulders slumped. "If I go to Hell, I'll never be able to return even if I do prove my innocence."

"Probably not, and be honest here, do you really want to?" he prodded.

She bit her lower lip before admitting, "Not really. I'd rather stay on Earth."

"Maybe we can find a way to make it happen. After all, you are my wife, and I do work there."

"I would like that I think, but at the same time, I want Theodore to be exposed. He shouldn't be allowed to hurt people."

"I'm sure he'll eventually get what's coming to him." And Julio hoped it involved his fist hitting that smug face numerous times.

Her lips turned down. "Will he? My Father, who has been complicit in Heaven, is all knowing, all seeing. And letting it happen."

"You said he's been imprisoned. Maybe this kind of behavior is more recent?" He didn't know why he tried to soften her disillusion.

"Maybe." Her shoulders rolled, but her expression remained morose.

"Come on. We should get out of here before the angels decide to ignore Hell's lawyer and take you by force." He held out his hand.

"I really don't want to go to Hell," was her stubborn reply.

"You say that, and yet you've never even seen it."

"I've seen images. It's brimstone and fire, torture and pain."

He snorted. "Brimstone, yeah, ashy also, but torture and pain? That's for those who deserve punishment. I promise, no one will hurt you." He meant it. He'd protect her from harm.

Hesitantly, she slid her fingers into his, and he drew her close, his cloak wrapping them in a black mist as he pulled on the magic that let him travel between the planes. With the angels gone, and their dampening spell with them, he could go wherever he liked. Including Hell.

He'd meant to go to the Guild; however, his path dumped them on the shore outside of the nine rings, the departure port for arriving souls. They milled around in snaking lines, lost souls dazed by their deaths, frightened by what their future held next.

"Fuck me, it's making us go the long way," he grumbled.

As a reaper, Julio refused to stand in any line. He took Helen to a pier where a boat bobbed, manned by a figure in a head-to-toe cloak. A skeleton hand gripped the long pole used to navigate and fight off the Styx monsters.

Helen breathed a name. "Charon."

The ferryman turned a faceless hood in their direction before shoving it back, showing off a freckled face with wild red hair. "Actually, the name's Clive. Charon's on vacation." He smiled, and Julio almost laughed at her expression.

"How can the Ferryman of Death take time off?" she asked, glancing back at all the waiting souls.

"Because his contract says he can. Last I heard, he was sailing on the *SS Sushimaker Two* Earth side with his son. Which is pretty brave. Adexios holds the record for sinking boats."

"Charon has a son." Stated with bemusement.

"I think you'll find Hell a lot different than you've been taught." Julio stepped into the boat, and she joined him, sitting primly on the bench, hands in her lap. Her wings, usually invisible, flickered into view. It drew a few gasps and one, "Holy shit, what did an angel do to deserve Hell?"

She replied, "I dared to question."

"What rule does that break?" Clive asked, half joking.

"It's number two, right after honor our Father, the almighty."

The boat set off, and despite her evident trepidation, Helen gazed around with curiosity at the water and the sky, which only lightly rained ash out over the Styx.

She held out her hands to catch a flake. "Where does it come from? What is burning?"

"It's from the furnace that keeps Hell warm. Without it, all this becomes an inhabitable frozen wasteland." It had happened before during an attack on the Dark Lord.

As they traversed the water, they drew attention from its denizens. Swells formed as shapes glided by, but it was the appearance of an eyestalk that startled her.

"What is that?" She leaned against Julio.

"One of the monsters. Mostly harmless," Clive announced but didn't add that they were harmless to the damned. The souls, already being dead, couldn't die again, but they could be hurt—or eaten. But what about an angel?

"Do they eat people?" she asked.

"Don't you worry, Miss Angel. I'll keep ya safe," Clive boasted, lifting his oar and twirling it to smack a creeping tentacle.

But while Clive fought off a big one, a tiny monster lifted itself on the gunwale and peered over with one giant bulbous eye, its skin a mottled mauve. It waved, and Helen waved back.

The baby monster gurgled, and she laughed. "It shouldn't be, but it is kind of cute."

The ferryman heard her. "I think it likes you."

She smiled as she petted the slimy head and said, "I like it, too."

And Julio liked Helen. A little too much. Something he suspected the moment the devil had suggested they get married and he didn't argue.

Him, a perpetual bachelor, tying the knot with an angel. But the worst part?

He didn't want a divorce.

17

HELL WAS nothing as Helen imagined. For one, it reminded her of a dirtier version of Earth.

As they neared the massive pier, she could see in the distance buildings, roads, people.

Demons, too.

They looked like she'd been told with horns and leathery skin. Claws and big teeth. What she didn't expect was for them to wear pants and have conversations. Some pushed carts; others threw out ropes to help dock the boats. A fellow with green skin offered her a hand to get out.

"Thank you," she said.

"Bah," the demon grunted.

As Julio landed beside Helen, she found herself leaning into his presence, comforted by it. She felt safe with him.

To her surprise, a red carpet suddenly unrolled and ended by her toes. The busy workers on the dock stayed clear of it, and the reason became obvious as she noticed the figure treading it in her direction.

Lucifer arrived wearing a military-style uniform heavy with medals. She could have sworn she heard bugles announcing his approach.

He stopped before her and beamed, appearing genuinely happy as he said, "Welcome to Hell."

"It's only temporary." She felt it necessary to say.

"Sure, it is. That's what they all say, but once you've had a taste of the circles, I guarantee you'll never want to go back up there." Lucifer rolled his eyes upward. "Given you're my guest, I've arranged for accommodations at the most luxurious condo overlooking the Styx."

"That's very kind of you," she said. "Thanks."

Whereas Julio snorted. "Don't be sucked in by this act. He wants something from you."

The devil spun his head as he kept walking, very disconcerting. "I want what we all want, for Helen to tell the truth to everyone in Heaven. Exoneration is the end goal. She can't exactly bask in that victory if she's dead."

Blunt. Harsh. Worse? She couldn't even deny the possibility. Theodore had made it clear he'd kill her. And for what? Because she saw him intimate with another angel. A rule and ban that made no sense. Why couldn't angels love each other?

"How long will I have to stay here?" she asked.

"Well, that depends on a few things," the devil said. "How long do you think that pompous prick can hold a grudge?"

She bit her lip. "A long time." Not the worst thing, she realized, and more of a relief. She wouldn't have to leave any time soon. She smiled at Julio, only to see him frowning.

"I can't stay, though. I'm supposed to be running Grim Dating," Julio declared.

"I'm sure you can commute." The devil waved his hand as if that would rid them of the problem.

"And leave her alone?" Julio shook his head.

"The angels wouldn't dare come after me here. Would they?" She looked at the devil for confirmation.

The sly demon in his suave male guise grinned with a dimple. "An angel would never set foot here intentionally."

She almost pointed out she'd agreed to come, but the devil had climbed into a strange carriage drawn by winged horses. If horses had manes of flame, burning eyes, and jutting, jagged teeth. When their cloven hoofs stamped impatiently at the ground, sparks scattered.

"We're riding in that?" she asked.

"I'm sure it's perfectly safe," was Julio's skeptical reply.

Whereas the devil laughed. "Never safe. Good thing I can't die. But don't worry, maybe if you croak, you'll be lucky and not come back as a bug."

"As usual, Dark Lord, your speeches are inspiring," Julio muttered with a snort and an eye roll.

Helen giggled then slapped her hand over her mouth lest the devil note her amusement at his insult. Surely the lord of Hell would smite Julio on the spot. Punish him. Put him in solitary for days. Years.

The devil laughed. "I am a master of linguistics. I've had centuries to perfect it. And yet, do I have time to impart my grand wisdom by penning the most epic story of all time? I don't, and so I inspire humans to write for me. Venerate me. Tell my story." The Dark Lord's expression turned devious. "The variations of me are plentiful. For I am legion."

A rumble went through the carriage as it lurched into motion, and Helen clung to Julio. Slightly frightened, as she realized the affable man before her was probably the deadliest thing in the universe, because her Father, who might be senile in Heaven, wasn't known to be a great fighter. Father God relied on his wits, and those had been declining.

Perhaps Charlie's takeover wasn't a bad thing. Now if only he'd do something. Imprisoning his Father meant he had the power. He should use it to bring Heaven into a more modern and just time. Starting by removing the sterilization of the female angels.

Not fair. Not right. Every angel should have a choice. Personally, Helen would avoid the whole baby-making thing because she'd yet to see the benefit of shoving a watermelon-sized creature from her moist areas.

Nasty. Although the way they were made through fornication intrigued, especially since that kiss in the chair. It was probably hugely sinful to want more.

She glanced at Julio and caught his eye. His smile warmed her, and she quivered inside when he squeezed her hand. Made her tingle. Hot.

Reminded her she wasn't alone.

If she went back to Heaven, she would have to give him up.

She really didn't want to. She wanted more time with Julio because her time on Earth had shown her that living creatures, human and not, craved affection. Desired to be touched.

I want love.

In Heaven, an empty spot gaped within her. Despite being in the most perfect place, she didn't feel happy. Barely even content. But it was her life. It was safe.

Until it wasn't.

At first, the new reality of Earth terrified, but as she navigated and learned, she found the hole within being filled. She felt happiness. If smiling and joy were a sin, then perhaps Heaven was the wrong place for her.

Curiosity as to other options was why she didn't fight her descent to Hell very hard. Earth turned out to be nothing like she'd been taught, and as it turned out, neither was Hell.

Even better, Hell had Julio.

Their conveyance stopped without mishap, and the door to the carriage opened. The devil swept a hand. "I'd love to stay and chat, but I need to check the children. Their mother has them this morning, along with a nanny trained in the fighting arts. Just in case."

"You fear an attack?" Helen asked.

"Yes. It's my wife you see. She's not well. Not well at all," he grumbled. "And this is why I had to hide Muriel, only I couldn't keep her and her magic down forever. And Jujube is already stronger. What can I do? I love them both."

On that cryptic note, the devil left.

They were alone.

Julio leapt out first and turned to offer a hand. For a supposed minion of the devil, he had a courteous method. She took his hand and got a different peek at the place she'd been taught to fear.

In Heaven, they spent a lot of time solitary, contemplating stuff that she really had no interest in. On Earth, and now here in Hell, chaos reigned. Everywhere she turned she heard noise, saw color, felt life. It energized her in a way she'd never imagined. She wanted to see and touch everything.

They'd left the pier behind for a sidewalk comprised of cobblestones, each the size of a fist, tightly place together to form a boulevard that could have accommodated several people wide. Between it was a smooth street with light traffic. Demons—who looked rather human if one ignored the horns and occasional fang—rode what looked like Earth horses with wings. Plodding manticores pulled wagons because even Hell had to fix and replace things.

But who made the supplies? Because now that she knew Elyon didn't create the cherubs, she had to wonder about the rest.

As she craned to eye the building that loomed high into the clouds of ash overhead, she asked, "Did the devil make all this?"

"No, we have workers that do the building or manufacturing. Although some stuff is imported from Earth."

"Your society isn't slovenly in other words."

He snorted. "It's Hell, not a free ride. If you want something, you work for it."

"Or steal it."

"Stealing is still work."

Massive rusted doors inset with smoked glass slid open at their approach, and she assumed the mechanism was the same as that on Earth. Once she stepped through, she realized, as she glanced back, that small demons with tails and limbs that wrapped around a pole were the ones to slide it open and shut.

Julio caught her staring. "Machines don't always work like they're supposed to in Hell. Something about the laws of psychics not being stable. You'll see lots of modern amenities done in a rather physical way. Kind of like *The Flintstones*."

"The what?"

He blinked at her and smiled, a long thing that transformed his entire face into something soft for her. "It's a television show I think you'll like. I can explain the parts you don't understand."

It implied that they'd be spending more time together, which suited her just fine.

The lobby reminded her of the one in Bambi's building with a grand space broken up by soft lighting and a desk for the guard. Only in this case, the guard turned out to be a rather massive demon. Thick. Muscled. Fanged. His red eyes flicked in their direction, and a lip peeled back.

"Who are you? Where are you going?" The high-pitched squeak almost made her laugh.

"I am none of your fucking business, going to more

of none of your fucking business." Julio's profanity didn't bother her. Words were words. And his use gave a certain elegance to them.

"Aren't you a prize today. Good thing for you I knew you were coming. Probably before her because you're a selfish prick."

"Fuck you," Julio declared.

"Kiss my hairy arsehole."

Helen blinked. Especially as they erupted into laughter.

"What room does she have?" Julio asked when it died down.

"According to my instructions, the angel gets the penthouse. But there ain't nothing set aside for you."

"No need because I'm with her."

The guard snorted. "Like fuck you are. She's way too pretty for the likes of you."

Helen's mouth rounded. Pretty?

"This pretty angel is my wife, so put the word out that messing with her is messing with me."

"Married." The guard snorted. "My condolences."

"You're just jealous because, with your ugly mug, even your hand looks away when you jerk off."

"I hope she gives you clamhellia."

Julio's final reply was a finger.

Helen waited until they got into the elevator to whisper, "Is everyone going to be that vulgar and aggressive?"

He snorted. "I guess you missed the part where we were joking. We're usually worse. Baezel is one of my buds. We used to play poker every Sunday when I lived at the guild."

"It seems an odd way to express a friendship."

"I didn't know there was a proper way," he said as the elevator jolted during its ascent.

She glanced dubiously around her. "This doesn't feel very safe."

"Nothing in Hell is. But you get used to it. Elevators beat the stairs, trust me. The penthouse in this place is nothing to joke about."

"You've been here before?"

"Nope. Way above my pay grade. I saw a televised special about it. The bathtub in the master bedroom is like a plunge pool."

Given he seemed enthused about it, she couldn't wait to see.

The elevator stopped with a shudder, and the doors slid open. She emerged into a vast space, too vast it seemed. She grabbed hold of Julio as he stepped out. Immediately, his cloak and presence wrapped around her.

It took her a moment to absorb the details—the massive room with high ceilings and windows on every far wall and more furniture than she'd ever seen —before she said, "This is for me?"

"Yup."

"And who else?"

"Me if you're okay sharing."

For some reason that eased her tension. But she found herself annoyed, and it took her a moment to realize why before she blurted aloud, "Why does Hell have nicer things than Heaven?"

"Who says Heaven doesn't have them?"

She opened her mouth to deny it, only to say, "There are angels living in places like this, aren't there?"

"Even if there weren't, you have to admit this is way nicer than what you described."

She glanced at him. "I hate it when you point things like that out."

His lips quirked. "Funny how the truth in this conversation is the problem. Isn't your God all about not lying?"

The pinch of her lips acted as a reply. She moved into the space, taking in the details. The fluted chimney came down into an egg-shaped fireplace split in the middle to show off blue flames. Only as she neared did she notice it emitted cold air, not hot. It helped with the sweltering dry heat she'd experienced outside.

A large curved couch wrapped around part of the coldplace, smooth and cream colored. A counter flanked the other side. Beyond it was the kitchen.

Julio whistled as he opened the fridge. "Damn, you got a working one. Even better, you're being spoiled. Cold beer for me, and for the lady, a spiked lemonade."

"Sounds painful."

"It's delicious. Here." He handed her a bottle, and she took a sip to find it tangy and sweet with a bite.

"This is more of that fire water," she exclaimed, holding it out from her.

"It's called alcohol, Curls."

"Drinking is a sin."

"Are we still keeping count?" he asked, heading for the wide bank of windows. Once more, he uttered a low whistle. "Check this out."

As she stood by his side, gazing outward, she blinked. For one, she'd expected ashy clouds. After all, the windows remained dark, but the blackness was only because they looked upon a universe.

Sort of.

Peering out she saw the ball of Earth with its moon and planets and stars and sun. At the same time, within, and yet not, as if a mirage she could only see if looking a certain way, she saw Hell. Her mind sought to understand the inverted sphere of its existence—and failed.

Then there was a gray fog of nothing. Could it be the fabled Limbo?

Within, and not at the same time, were the rigid lines of Heaven. Lattice upon axis upon vertices.

That wasn't the end of it, though. There were more places of existence. Some purely made of liquid. Others of fire. Ice. Something she couldn't even name.

This couldn't be real.

She touched the glass, and the image in the window stabilized to that of Heaven. Zoomed in almost dizzyingly fast before hovering above the nursery. She'd never seen it from this angle, and yet she recognized it.

"What is that place?" Julio asked, standing behind her.

"That was my home." Did he notice her use of the past tense?

"Seems"—he cocked his head—"very clean."

"It is. Pristine and mostly white. Color is chaotic."

"I'm surprised you're allowed hair, skin, or eye color," he noted.

"That's not something that can be changed, although some nannies choose to shave their hair." She ran a hand over her curls. "I didn't because I like it."

"Me, too."

His words made her shy, and she ducked her head. "Hell is not what I expected."

"And you're not what I'd have expected either." He pulled her against him.

She tilted her head to keep their gazes locked. "Is it wrong I like being here with you?"

"You need to reevaluate your concept of right and wrong."

"How?"

"By experiencing things, because you ain't seen nothing yet." He dropped a light kiss on her lips, and her eyes closed in anticipation of more. Instead he tapped her buttocks and snapped, "Let's go exploring, Curls. I know a psychic who makes a mean souvlaki and can tell you your future at the same time."

The only future she wanted was standing right in front of her.

But she went exploring with him. Ate some of the best souvlaki. Met the very pregnant Sasha, who, at times, appeared to be arguing with someone she called the future. Sometimes she would spout vague things such as numbers at random, but she said the weirdest thing as they were leaving. "Don't let her swallow it."

Who swallow what?

Sasha the psychic never said.

As they walked back to the gate to return to the second ring, because only the devil's family or highly placed minions got the first, she held Julio's hand. Her heart full. Her lips pulled in a smile. This was happiness.

She'd turned to say something when she heard a strange sound overhead. A glance showed a long pink shape gliding past.

"What is that?" she exclaimed.

"Dragon."

"They don't exist."

"You just saw one. Care to rephrase?"

"But it was pink. In the stories they are green or gray, red only in fiction."

He snorted. "That's the devil's doing. He gave the pink dragon to his granddaughter. I hear his daughter Muriel was pissed. Apparently, the kid is a bit of an escape artist."

"The devil has more than one child? And a grand-child?" The concept was odd given Elyon only ever had the one son. Although she'd heard rumors after his imprisonment there might be another. And it wasn't an immaculate conception.

"He does have family, but rumor has it his kids don't live to be old. He kills them the moment they start coming after his throne."

"That's horrible."

"He's the devil," was his reply.

A devil who proved to be complex. Actually,

everyone she'd met had layers to them that made engaging with them fascinating. But the one that intrigued her most accompanied her into the home she'd been given in Hell.

Julio said, "You should have a bath."

She wrinkled her nose. "I'd prefer a quick shower." She enjoyed Earth's hot water that emerged from a spout rather than the cool basins for bathing in Heaven.

"You only think that because you've never been in a Jacuzzi plunge pool. Come on, I'll show you how it works."

He took her to a wall of windows, only for her to realize the windows slid aside to reveal a bathroom with a water hole in the floor.

Julio had shed his shoes already and dipped a toe in. "Perfect temperature."

She followed his example and, after removing her footwear, tested the surface of the water.

Hot.

Fragrant, too, she noticed, sniffing the steam.

"Get in."

Since he seemed insistent, she stepped down into it, noticing the stairs underwater.

Julio laughed. "You were supposed to take your clothes off first."

"But you're here."

"Bodies are a natural thing. Clothes aren't, or we'd be born with them."

The argument forced her to think. "Nudity is a sin."

What she fell back on since she didn't have a good rebuttal.

"I thought we'd agreed most of your rules are bullshit."

"If bodies are natural, then why are you dressed?" she blurted out.

"I thought you'd never ask." It didn't take him long to divest himself, but she stopped watching after the shirt came off and showed off the slabs of muscle across his chest. His cloak remained but was just a shadow at his back, that did nothing to hide his body.

A glimpse was enough, though, to heat her blood. She heard rather than saw him slip into the water. When she opened her eyes, it was to find him in front of her, a half-grin on his lips.

"Hey, Curls. You gonna get comfortable?"

"I'm fine," she lied. She wasn't okay. She throbbed between her legs. She wanted to reach for him. Wanted to ask for another kiss.

They were married now. Except for one thing. "We never consummated our vows."

His eyes widened. "No, we didn't."

"Isn't that part of the ritual to ensure the marriage can't be dissolved?" She'd seen it in a movie.

"Are you saying you want to have sex with me?"

The bold manner in which he asked had her suddenly shy. She licked her lips. "I think I would like it if you kissed me again."

He groaned as he swept her into his arms and plundered her mouth. The heat inside her ignited, as did a throbbing pleasure. She grabbed him and touched. Felt the skin of his broad shoulders and strong back. The firmness of his flesh.

Gasped as his hands divested her of her clothes. The water felt great nude. His stroking fingers felt even better.

She moaned into his mouth as he kissed her. Writhed as he touched her and made her yearn for something more.

Sin. Sin. Sin.

The word chanted inside her head, and yet she didn't care. She felt good and alive. Wanted more.

When he sat her on the edge of the tub, her eyes opened. He'd remained in the water, level with...

She blushed as he parted her. She put her hands against her mound.

He nudged them with his lips and said, "If you move them, I can make you feel really good."

"Better than I feel now?" she asked.

"So fucking good."

Such sinful promise in that claim. She placed her hands on the stone rim of the tub and closed her eyes before he touched her.

With his mouth. Down there.

She cried out. Her hips bucked. Only once and then he held her. Gripped her as he kissed her below and made her writhe with pleasure. Squirm against her need.

When that peak of ecstasy hit, she cried out, and her body undulated. He wasn't done.

He licked her and pushed fingers against her, the strangeness of it drawing pants. He emerged from the water, sleek and wet, his expression smoldering hunger.

She understood that hunger. She kissed him and pressed her body to his. He grabbed her around the waist and carried her to the couch, where he lay her down before he covered her with his frame.

His lips sought hers. His hand went between their bodies and stroked.

Soon she writhed under him, moaning and panting. Needing something.

She stilled as something hard pressed against her. Her eyes opened, and she met his gaze.

Intent, yet he paused.

She put her arms around his neck and drew him close for a kiss as he pushed into her. She cried out at a sharp pain. There and gone, erased by a spreading pleasure as he filled her.

Literally. She could feel him inside her, and she quivered.

He groaned. "Fuck me, Curls. If you do that again, I might come too quick."

"Do what?" She shuddered, squeezing him.

He uttered a sound and began to move inside her, and she cried out. Dug her fingers into his shoulders as he thrust his hardness into her. Stretched her and struck at something that made her tighten.

Until she exploded and found herself floating above herself but not alone. He was there in that moment, surrounding her with his warmth.

When she came back to herself, she remained warm and snug in his arms.

He kissed her lightly. "Guess that makes our marriage official."

"Meaning what?" she asked.

"I'm not letting you go. And anyone that tries to take you will get a fight."

The promise had her kissing him again. The hunger she now understood as lust filling her.

They didn't make it to the bed. The coldplace bathed their heated skin as she sat atop him, rocking her hips, sinning in the most delightful way.

His hands touched her all over.

Her fingers dug into his chest as she found true heaven.

In his arms.

18

JULIO WAS IN LOVE. With an angel, of all things.

Fucking crazy. He knew it, and yet he couldn't help it. Something about Helen sucked him in, and he didn't intend to fight to escape. He wanted to remain married. It might have been done under duress to save her, but he wanted it to be real.

Had hope she might want to stay with him as well.

Not once since her arrival had she mentioned going back to Heaven. He'd seen her curiosity as they explored Hell. Everything was new and wondrous to her, but at the same time, she learned quickly. Especially when it came to pleasing him. She already knew how to make him feel good in bed and out. His happiness just needed her around.

Ugh. What kind of sappy bullshit was infecting his mind?

He couldn't help but jump on the chance to clear his head when a call came in from Grim Dating. Apparently, there was a client demanding to speak to the commander. Given the boss was still on vacation, that meant Julio.

Helen was in the kitchen, banging around. She had no idea how to cook but was keen on learning.

She smiled at him, and he just about took her on the counter right then and there. He'd done it before, her legs wrapped around his waist, the welcoming heat of her snug around his shaft. By the time there were done fucking, he'd been somehow ended up wearing her halo on a tilt, and she wore the grin of orgasmic satisfaction. It made eating her attempts at cooking worth it.

"I gotta pop into the office to handle something. Will you be okay?"

Helen nodded and plopped a strange fruit onto the counter, along with an onion. "I've got a new recipe to try."

"Yay. Can't wait." He might bring them back some donuts just in case.

He kissed her, slipped in some tongue, then thought, *Fuck it*, and fingered her until she gasped into his mouth.

Julio left, his smug smile stretching ear to ear. It was quickly wiped as he stepped into the boss's office and saw who waited for him.

"Michael." The archangel. One of the biggest and baddest supposedly. Also, a client who was going through dating options faster than a teenage boy with a bottle of lotion.

Given the ease Michael managed to get panties off women, it made Julio wonder why he bothered with

Grim Dating. He didn't need help getting pussy, which meant the archangel had another reason for always coming around.

Michael offered him a bright smile, his teeth matching the white glare of his suit. "Julio, just the man I wanted to see. I hear you have something that belongs to Heaven, and I'm here to ask that you give it back."

Julio did his best to not react. He also knew better than to play stupid. "I don't know that Helen would agree she belongs in Heaven, given the issues she's had with one of your soldiers. He tried to kill her because she caught him fucking a nanny."

The declaration didn't surprise Michael, who had a ready answer. "I'm aware of the situation with Theodore, and it is being handled. The unpleasantness is why I chose to come here and announce that, given the circumstances, all charges against Helen have been dropped. She can come home."

Julio's stomach just about bottomed out. Helen leave? It would be selfish to ruin that chance for her.

Good thing he wasn't a nice guy.

"I doubt you'll want her back. You do know we're married, and when I say married, I mean *very married*." He purred the last with as much innuendo as possible.

"Coerced into marriage. I'm pretty sure she can be forgiven this one time given the situation." Michael offered a conspiratorial smile. "Rest assured, we have ways of ensuring she forgets her sins and returns to a life of chastity and goodness."

At the claim, Julio wrinkled his nose. Helen deserved better than that. And he'd meant it when he said he wouldn't let her go. "Pretty sure my marriage vows stated 'til death do us part."

"Is that meant to be a temptation? Because my sword, unlike the human version, will kill a reaper." The angel drew a gleaming length of metal but of a kind not seen on Earth or in Hell.

Could it harm him? Julio would prefer to not find out.

"Why are you so determined to have her back? I know she's broken too many rules for you to ignore."

"As I said, extenuating circumstances have led to us being lenient. Do not judge us on the actions of one. Helen belongs to us, and you will return her," Michael stated lightly, but Julio recognized the threat.

"No, not to mention she's pissed you lied. She doesn't want to go back."

"We'll deal with it." Michael twirled his sword.

"Yeah, still not handing her over."

"I didn't figure you would," Michael said, lifting his gaze from his twirling blade to smirk at Julio. "Which is why I made other plans."

The cold in Julio's veins manifested his sudden fear. "You can't touch her. You and I both know angels wouldn't dare set foot in Hell."

"No, they wouldn't. But the thing about demons and the damned is they have few scruples. Just about anyone can be bought for the right price."

The fear turned to ice. "You wouldn't dare attack her while she's in Lucifer's care."

"I wouldn't, but the demons I bribed did." Michael

pointed to his watch. "As we speak, they're acquiring Helen."

"No." Julio swirled his cloak to open a portal, only to have Michael shoot out a hand and grab at the esoteric fabric.

The angel somehow locked him in place and, in that same low, even tone, said, "It's already too late. And let me add that you will not come after her. If you are seen anywhere near the pearly gates, you will die."

"Halo fucker. You can forget using Grim Dating as your personal bootie call center." Julio's mature reply as the angel left. He hoped Michael saw the finger he flashed.

It wasn't until the angel left the building that he could finally call a portal. He stepped through the rip and found the penthouse a mess. Yet that wasn't the most astonishing thing.

The big surprise was the pink dragon sitting inside.

19

BEFORE THE DRAGON ARRIVED...

The moment Julio left, Helen missed him. She'd gotten used to having him around. Quite enjoyed it and almost asked to join him at the office.

She also wondered if she should have time alone. A moment with only herself and her thoughts to see if it was his presence making her reject a lifetime of teaching.

Being with Julio was nothing like she'd ever experienced. She didn't want it to end. Cringed at the thought of returning to her sterile and lonely life in Heaven.

Not that it seemed likely any more at this point. She'd discovered a whole wide world existed with rules she could abide by. She could laugh. Smile.

Love...

Could it be possible? Did an angel love a denizen of Hell?

Not long after Julio left, the elevator rattled back up

to their floor. The doors opened just as her thumbs pierced the skin of the fruit she needed to peel. She glanced over and expected to see Julio. Perhaps even Baezel, who sometimes brought packages delivered to reception from the stores where Julio had insisted she buy trinkets. Such as an apron, which she currently wore.

Even Lucifer or Bambi appearing wouldn't have surprised her. Both had randomly visited since her arrival, although neither stayed long. She had to admit the Dark Lord didn't look so dark when he had a small child on his shoulders who grinned and waved before grabbing hold of Lucifer's hair. Obviously painful and yet the devil bore it with stoic grace.

None of those familiar faces spilled from the elevator. Instead, she was visited by three massive demons, their olive-green skin dry and mottled. Their tusks yellowed. Eyes baleful and glowing.

They growled and grunted in her direction. Not a good sign.

She tugged her thumb stuck in the fruit someone called a Hellange. It refused to let it go, so she gave it a violent shake and sent it flying. A demon lifted his hand and grabbed it with a chuckle that turned into a scream as he began to smoke.

Helen glanced at the other piece of fruit and the ingredients that she'd blessed out of habit. Holy food.

To fight demons.

She fisted another ingredient and threw. Missed. The demons caught on to her plan and rushed for her. In desperation she ran for the window and yelled, "In the name of my Father—who has some explaining to do—his son Charlie, and the Holy Spirit that moved me last night, I need someone to rescue me. Amen."

As a hand reached and grabbed at her hair, drawing a sharp scream, she saw something outside. Rescue came in the form of a crash as a massive pink dragon slammed into a window and ended up inside her living room.

The demon at her back, distracted, released her.

The pastel-colored beast shook its head, scattering shards, and Helen covered her head as they flew with sharp bite.

She heard a yell and a juicy crunch that strongly suggested she keep her eyes closed. A grunt, followed by more wet chewing.

Then the ding of the elevator.

She didn't peek until she heard Julio exclaim, "Curls, where are you?"

Opening her eyes, she discovered herself behind the massive dragon where he couldn't see her. She walked around and waved. "I'm here. I'm okay." So long as the dragon contented itself with eating the now very dead demons. She didn't know why those demons had attacked and could only fall back on her lessons that claimed evil thrived on violence.

She did her best to ignore the blood. Julio didn't care and strode through the mess to sweep her into a hug that squeezed and lifted her off the floor.

She squealed.

He buried his face against her. "I'm glad you're still here."

"Me, too."

The dragon gagged. A startled glance in its direction showed it waddling away. As it leaped out through an unbroken window, Julio nuzzled her cheek.

"You okay, Curls?"

"I am now." She kissed him, but he soon controlled it, his mouth insistent on hers, his hands pulling her into him. Imprinting the strength of him on her.

She embraced him just as fervently. Mouth hot and demanding. She couldn't get enough. The clothes were about to come off when the devil arrived.

20

THERE WAS something strangely satisfying about interrupting people on the verge of fucking. Lucifer basked in their exasperation, inhaled their throbbing need. Their frustration tickled.

Delicious shit.

However, not the reason why he'd interrupted a promising couple from consummating. Much as he'd like to see Heaven choke on Helen's choice, it was time for the next phase of his plan.

"Hello, Reaper."

"Go the fuck away."

Lucifer *tsked*. "That is not the correct way to greet me if you're going to keep your man parts, my friend."

With a grumble, Julio released Helen and faced the devil. "Evening, dark lord, how can I fucking help you?"

"That's better. A little heavy on the insolence, but then again, all my best soldiers seem to have a bit too much of a backbone."

"I assume there's a reason for your visit." Which,

when translated, was actually, "Tell me what you want then fuck off."

"I'm afraid the fucking will have to wait, Reaper, so tuck away your little friend. I have to admit to surprise that you'd want to waste time doing the horizontal tango given what just happened. The lovely Helen was attacked and this after I'd extended my personal protection to her as my guest. Some demons have a lot of nerve!" the devil exclaimed. "A shame the dragon took care of them. I'd have loved to torture them myself."

"You can still go after the one who hired them," Julio stated. "And send a warning to anyone else who thinks it's okay to come after Helen."

The boy had gotten sharp since he'd come to Hell. No more haze from the drugs and booze. He'd gone clean. Lucifer, though, knew how to talk his way in circles. "What makes you think they were hired?"

"Because I was talking to Michael the archangel, and he told me he'd bribed demons to take her!" Julio raked his fingers through his hair while Helen remained quiet and listening. Frowning as well.

"Michael sent them?" she suddenly asked. "*The* Michael?"

Julio pressed his lips and nodded.

"That's who you went to meet?"

Julio sighed. "I didn't know until I got there."

"What did he want?" she asked.

The devil snorted. "What do you think he wanted?"

"Me?" Her voice emerged low and soft.

Julio nodded. "Michael told me to hand you over."

"That's not all he said," Lucifer the troublemaker sang. "Tell her all of it."

That had the reaper scowling. "He said he'd taken care of Theodore and you'd be forgiven. That you could return to Heaven."

Helen's expression froze. "But I don't want to."

Relief flood Julio's face. "I didn't think you did, which is why I said no, a couple of times as a matter of fact. He then said it didn't matter because he'd hired someone to kidnap you while I was distracted."

"Only he didn't count on Lucinda's dragon to come to the rescue." Lucifer clapped his hands.

"How did the dragon get up here?" Julio asked.

"I don't know," Lucifer lied. No need to tell them about a certain foretelling. His seer had been on a roll lately, predicting all kinds of cool shit if paths were nudged a certain way. Why he might even be able to do something about the Jujube-Gaia situation if he tweaked events just right. "Does it really matter how the dragon got up here? The thing we should focus on is the attack on Helen." Lucifer diverted their attention.

"It happened because the security guard on duty sucks." Julio scowled.

"Security was getting blown in the closet." Lucifer had watched for a bit before interrupting another couple about to have sex.

"What are you going to do to fix this so it doesn't happen again?" Julio growled.

"Me? How is this my problem?"

"You said it yourself, she's your guest. What are you going to do to protect her?"

"Replace you for starters, apparently. If anyone is to blame, it's you. Leaving her alone." Lucifer shook his head in disappointment. "And here I thought you'd protect her."

Julio's jaw clenched. "I know how to protect her. We need to clip some wings. Those angels need to accept she's not going back."

"Technically, they are well within their right to demand her return. We do have an agreement, you know."

"Which they broke."

"Did they?" Lucifer asked. "You brought an angel to Hell."

"And? She's not the first. Your own daughter is married to an angel," Julio pointed out.

"The difference is Helen has not yet fallen."

Julio's face creased in confusion. "How can she not be? She's broken a ton of their rules."

"Newer rules. Not the old ones. The ones that count most. And being fallen is more than just the breaking of their laws. My brother has to actually cast an angel out if they're going to be blocked from Heaven. And we all know that's not going to happen anytime soon given his sabbatical."

"I'm not fallen?" Helen asked.

"Nope. And until you are, you're considered a citizen of Heaven. Which is causing all kinds of legal problems. We've been managing to stall them because of the whole marriage thing. However, without progeny involved, they're already speaking of dissolving the union. A full annulment."

"They can't annul. We've consummated," Julio said, and Helen squeaked.

"Doesn't matter. Angels cannot marry. Especially not a reaper created with my power."

Julio growled. "There has to be a loophole."

The devil shrugged. "We're working on it. Ideally, my brother gets out of whatever prison Charlie has him held in and he begins dealing fallen status like cards in a poker game."

"How long before that happens?" Julio asked.

"Depends on which future we're talking about. Most of them it's a few centuries. In some, he never gets out, and boy, talk about angels gone wild." Lucifer slapped his leg.

"Meaning it's not going to happen anytime soon."

Helen put a hand on Julio's arm. "The devil is here because he has an idea, though."

"Clever girl." Lucifer winked.

Whereas the reaper glared. "Oh no you don't. You're not using Helen in whatever weird plot you have brewing."

"Me, plot?" Lucifer might have exaggerated a tad. He'd been out of sorts lately. It didn't help his wife suddenly played perfect mother to the children. He'd gone from being their primary caretaker to having to hunt them down, certain she'd finally flipped, only to find them doing something wholesome. Like baking cookies shaped like horned ducks. Or making him that cooling blanket in the shape of a shark eating him.

"Knowing you, you're going to dangle her like bait." Julio knew him so well.

But the devil knew Julio even better.

"On the contrary, I want Helen to stay out of Heaven. Why do you think I've been avoiding the phone calls?" Each communication was getting more strident in demand. Lucifer had heard from a few of the major archangels at this point, Michael being the most irritating. None of the demands came from his brother. Nor Charlie. No one had seen his nephew since after he'd had his Father imprisoned.

What the fuck was happening in Elyon's kingdom?

"You can't hand her over. If I'd have known she could be in danger, I wouldn't have left her alone!" Julio simmered. Even Helen's hand on his arm didn't calm him. The reaper had a soft spot for the angel. "Why didn't you warn me the angels could bribe someone?"

"You made the mistake of assuming the angels had scruples. They are masters when it comes to manipulating the rules to suit themselves."

"Meaning she's not safe and will need better protection." Julio eyed Lucifer so he had to set him straight.

"Do I look like a fucking bodyguard?" the devil asked softly.

"No, Dark Lord." Julio dipped his head.

"Even if I were to assign a legion for her protection, it wouldn't be enough. The angels have made it clear they want Helen back."

"Too bad, so sad. Not happening," Julio stated.

"What about what Helen wants?" The devil turned to her. "Tell me, little angel, do you want to go back to Heaven? You still can."

Her lips parted. "Go home?"

"They'll kill her." Julio huffed.

"Why does it matter to you what happens to her?" the devil asked, and he wasn't the only one who stared at Julio for an answer.

Julio lifted his chin. "It matters 'cause she's my wife. And I'll not let anyone reap her soul."

Helen liked the answer enough her arms went around Julio's midsection and she hugged him. Julio's arm and cloak curled around her protectively.

"Tell us what we can do to keep Helen safe." Julio fell into Lucifer's trap.

Wearing his finest salesman smile, Lucifer said, "I'm glad you asked, because I have an idea that helps us both. Your problem is you need to go somewhere no one can find you, and lucky you, I know just the place."

With a theatrical swirl that got no love, Lucifer had them standing in what remained of the eighth ring, now only a few strides wide. The fog creeping and stealing land showed no signs of slowing.

Was it time to check on the source of the issue himself? To venture into the mist that none returned from?

Nah. That was what minions existed for.

Julio took one look at the roiling fog and shook his head. "You want us to go in there? Are you fucking nuts? I've heard no one who enters ever comes out."

Lucifer shrugged. "Thus far it's been an issue, but given you're both special, and determined, I know you can fix it."

"Why the fuck would I agree to a suicide mission?" Julio snapped.

"Because if you succeed in finding and stopping this fog that's eating my kingdom, I'll bestow upon your angel my official Satanic blessing and solve your Heaven problem."

"Why not just give it to her?"

"Because you mistake me for someone benevolent and kind. You scratch my hairy back, I'll scratch yours. Piss me off, and I'll set you on fire. Not to mention, you both owe me a favor, and I'm calling it."

Helen ventured to ask, "Is it dangerous?"

"Undoubtedly." Lucifer smiled, his best shark version. "No one has returned yet, but I believe in you." One of these times when he said it, it would actually be true.

"Fuck you. You have no idea what's in there." Julio bristled.

Helen tilted her face to look at Julio. "You don't have to go."

"If we don't, then you'll be hunted."

"Exactly. It's me they're after. Maybe I should just turn myself in," Helen offered.

Lucifer almost gagged at the martyr act. It pissed off Julio, too.

"Shut up, Curls." Julio growled. "I'll handle this."

Wrong choice of words.

Lucifer conjured some popcorn to watch the fireworks as Helen found her spine and said, "I won't shut up. Because, apparently, I don't have to. That fog is too dangerous. I won't have you hurt because of me."

Lucifer took a sip of soda and a bite of licorice as she called Julio's bravery into question.

"You think I'm afraid?" Julio's cloak swirled in agitation. "I fear nothing. I'm already dead. It's just a mist."

"If it's so benign, then why are you refusing to enter it?" Lucifer taunted, joining the argument.

Julio glared. "I was busting your balls."

"Not very well. Didn't feel a thing," Lucifer declared. A good ball busting would have had him cringing. Gaia knew how to have them hurting so good. He'd miss her when the babies sent her over sanity's edge. It had happened before, although with Muriel, it took a few years before she snapped. Mother Nature didn't handle postpartum very well.

"If I go into this fucking fog, will you go the fuck away?" barked Julio.

"You really need to work on your ass-kissing skills because my hairy buttocks are not feeling any love. And you should really make up your minds because this"—the devil held up a cellphone that rang stridently—"is Heaven calling again and one guess as to what they're going to demand." The phone calls always started with a demand for Lucifer's capitulation to Heaven. He'd refuse, it would get ugly, and usually it ended in Heaven hanging up with the angel on the other end claiming they needed to bleach their ears.

Julio sliced a hand through the air. "We're not handing Helen to the angels. Or going into that deadly fog. Have you never read that Stephen King short story titled 'The Mist'?"

"Saw the movie and the miniseries. Do you think he's behind it?" Lucifer brightened at the thought. He did so love a good horror story.

"I don't think we have a choice," Helen softly said. She glanced at the mist. "I guess the question is, will the fog kill us?"

"I don't know." Lucifer shrugged. "Let's ask my eight ball." He pulled it from a pocket and gave it a shake. "Looking cloudy with a chance of showers."

"Could you give a straight answer for once?" Julio grumbled. "I'd just like to know if I'm going to die in the next thirty seconds."

Lucifer shrugged. "No idea. I can't see inside that space. It's hidden from me. You might stop existing the moment you step in, fall into a pond of liquid shit, or you could end up in paradise."

"And this is supposed to convince us to go in?" was Julio's sarcastic drawl.

Helen grabbed Julio's hand. "I have faith."

"In what? And if you say your Father..." Julio threatened.

Her lips twisted in wry amusement. "I was going to say I have faith in you, in us."

Julio sighed. "Fuck me, we're an us. Guess we're doing this together. Ready, wife?"

She nodded.

"Let's go."

Julio pulled her into the mist, and Lucifer could sense them no more.

Fuck a duck.

He really hoped they hadn't bitten the dust.

21

A GOOD THING Julio held on to Helen, because two steps in and they were enveloped. Smothered head to toe in fog, sightless, soundless. The falling ash stopped. Only mist loomed all around, and he'd have sworn it cried out, which was really disturbing even to someone like him. It was solid underfoot, and yet he couldn't clearly see the ground. The smoky air covered it.

What was happening here? Why did it feel so... dead? No, dead wasn't right. He knew death. This place had a nothing feel to it. As if empty of everything.

And he didn't like it one bit.

"Julio?" Helen's clutched at him, the only thing of substance, and he welcomed the touch.

He drew her close, and his cloak flared around them, clearing a space. "I'm here."

"I'm scared. This place... It feels wrong. Did we die?"

He wanted to say no, but he stuck to the truth. "I don't know."

"What should we do?"

"The only thing we can if we want the Dark Lord's help. We have to find the source of the fog."

"How big is this mist?" she asked as they walked through the gloomy space.

"I'm not sure. I expect it to be pretty vast. The fog started in the Wilds and seems to have swallowed part of Hell's eighth ring and all of its ninth."

"So we're in Hell?"

"Maybe?" Not exactly a great reply.

"If I had to guess, I'd say no," she mused aloud.

"Why?" he asked even as he agreed.

"It doesn't have the same feel."

"Meaning?"

She rolled her shoulders. "In Hell, there is a certain hot vibrancy in the air. So many smells and textures. Living chaos."

"So, this place is more like Heaven?"

She shook her head. "Not exactly. In Heaven, it's sterile smells and smooth spaces. Organization and structure. This place… it's as if it has yet to decide what it wants to be. As if it is the absence of all. You said it began in a wild place?"

"That's the assumption. Beyond the ninth ring used to be the Wilds, an unclaimed land with no ruler, no end. At first, it appeared to be the thing creeping in on Hell. Then one day, the fog appeared and swallowed it." Saying it aloud he had to wonder, did the fog eat? Were they currently being digested? Here was hoping it didn't shit them out somewhere worse.

Rather than ponder if he'd end up excreted into a

latrine, he walked hand in hand with Helen for a long time.

A long.

Long.

Time.

Long enough he finally growled in frustration.

"There's nothing here." Nothing to sight on. Nothing to explore. They could be moving in circles and never know.

"There has to be something in here somewhere." She leaned into him, tucked under his cloak. In this place, he wasn't about to let her go. They might never find each other again.

"I think we should take a break," he suggested.

"Here?"

"You know of a better spot?"

She shook her head. As she crossed her legs to sit, his cloak slithered to land beneath her and spread to accommodate them both. He lay on his side by her, comfortable enough to put his hand on her belly, knowing she wanted to talk by the expression on her face.

"What happens if we can't find anything?" she asked.

"I don't know. I can't call a doorway." He'd tried. Something jammed his access.

"We're stuck with no supplies. Will we get hungry?" She asked some of the same questions he pondered with no answer.

To his surprise, she was the one to offer comfort as

she whispered, "At least we're together." Then she kissed him. Touched him. Demanded his passion.

They made love in that nothing place, him on the bottom watching her as she rode him, her wings flaring with a silver glint as she came.

His angel.

His wife.

"I love you," he whispered as she snuggled in his arms after her climax.

"I love you, too." Whispered a moment before she fell asleep and he soon followed.

Julio didn't know how long he rested before he woke. Helen squirmed to get out from under his arm and cloak.

"What's wrong?" he asked, groggy still.

"Apparently, even in a nowhere place, I have to void myself."

He snorted. "Then that makes two of us."

"Where am I supposed to do it?" she asked.

"On the ground."

"Where we slept?" she asked in shock.

"Yup. It's what you do when there's no toilet. Try not to splash your feet."

The noise she uttered had him chuckling. "It's not that bad. Here's something to wipe with." He tore a strip from his shirt.

She eyed him and the fabric then sighed. "Don't watch."

"I'd rather not lose you because I took my eyes off you."

She grimaced.

"How about I stand right behind you, facing away, would that help? I'll pee, too, if it makes you feel better."

"Not really. You're much better equipped than I am for projectile fluid release."

He chuckled. "Do you have penis envy, Curls?"

"No! Although it is rather remarkable."

His chest swelled. "You're the one who is amazing." Funny how quickly he'd come around to liking his angel. To loving her.

"I shall void, but you shan't watch. And that goes for your cloak, too."

"Fine. But stay near."

Back to back, they pissed on the ground, or so he assumed since he still couldn't see his feet, but in good news they didn't end up in a warm puddle. It was the first time since their arrival that they weren't touching.

As he finished up and started to zip, he heard her say, "Do you hear that?"

"Hear what, Curls?" He finished straightening his clothes and turned around to see her walking away from him, her head canted.

"That song. It's beautiful."

"Where are you going, Curls?" He reached for her, but she slipped through his grasp before he got hold.

"I have to find it."

He still couldn't hear whatever sparked her interest, but his cloak must have sensed something amiss because it fluttered and rippled at his back, agitated. He aimed it for Helen, and the edge of it curled around her ankle.

Helen paused and turned a puzzled expression in his direction. "It stopped."

"What about now?" he asked. On a hunch, he removed his cloak from her leg.

"It's calling me. I must answer." She took a step, and he grabbed her again. Worried.

Once more she halted. "I can't hear it anymore."

"I think my cloak disrupts whatever spell is in this place." It would explain why he remained unaffected.

She chewed her lower lip. "Maybe I should follow it."

"No." He didn't want her bespelled. But on the other hand...

"We have to. It's the only clue we've got to possibly get out of here. Just be sure to keep me in sight." She shoved free of his cloak.

He didn't have to ask if she heard anything. She began to walk again, faster this time. He took long strides to keep her in sight, but he didn't grab her. Whatever siren song she heard didn't affect him, but she was correct. While he hated using her as a lodestone, it gave them a direction finally in this sightless and soundless place.

They didn't have to go far as it turned out.

Without warning, in a spot where the fog was so thick he could barely see his hand in front of him, she dropped to her knees. The space in front of her was clear as she reached for a strange sphere, no bigger than a lemon, buried in the smooth ground. It pulsed, the waves of it wrong, discordant. Soundless. Lightless. Yet vibrating Julio's very essence.

Before she could touch it, he wrapped his cloak around her, snapping her out of the spell.

She took in a deep breath. "That was very strange."

"Has it stopped talking to you?"

She leaned her head. "Not entirely. Can't you hear it?"

This close to the object, he could, faintly, but he ignored it. "I don't know what that thing is, but it feels wrong."

"It wants me to touch it." She hummed softly.

Before Julio could stop Helen, she leaned away from him and placed a hand on it. Immediately, her body went rigid. Her head fell back hard enough it knocked her halo askew.

Not liking that one bit, he whipped his cloak around her even more securely, hoping to counter the spell. It did nothing, so he used his arms, hugging and tugging her backwards.

She whispered, "It wants me."

"What does?" he asked as he tried to peel her away.

"The egg. It needs."

"Needs what?" he asked, grunting as he pulled harder and got nowhere.

"Me." She cast him a glance, her expression drawn.

Her statement had him on his knees, renewing his efforts to remove her hand from the egg, but it was as if it were glued in place. No amount of yanking freed her hand, and she began to moan, leaning forward as if being drawn into the stone, the lines of her body blurring.

Panicked, he pulled forth his stave, which appeared

dull in this gray, lifeless place. Being careful of the hand cradling it, Julio jammed the pointed end into the egg, and it emitted an angry wave, hard enough that Helen fell back with a gasp.

Julio immediately wrapped his cloak around her as he faced off against the sphere, which began to pulse visibly enough to be seen. And heard. Its jangling scream brought a wince.

Which was when he decided enough was enough. He raised his weapon and brought it down, only to have it bounce off the hard surface.

The blow angered the egg. It vibrated faster, putting out a call even he could almost hear. Entities answered its siren pulse, suddenly rushing in from the mist. An imp that leaped into the egg and was absorbed with an ecstatic cry. Then a damned soul.

The egg acted as a vortex, sucking them in. An alien thing that had no place here in Hell or anywhere and he had no idea how to stop it.

Meanwhile more bodies hurtled through the mist, all on foot, but it was from above the largest beast appeared. A giant pink dragon circled overhead. Perhaps it would save Helen again.

The dragon dove for the sphere, and as it arrowed, he heard a squeal. A second later, he saw the child perched on the beast's back.

"No. Turn away. It's dangerous." Julio waved his arms, knowing who the little person had to be.

Lucifer's granddaughter. He couldn't let the egg swallow her.

The dragon opened its mouth and inhaled.

Oh fuck.

He wasn't sure what the handbook said about reapers getting engulfed in dragon breath. Didn't really want to find out.

Julio grabbed Helen and dove with her, covering her body with his as they hit the ground. He waited to be crisped by the dragon.

Instead he heard a light thump. A peek showed the beast had landed, and Lucinda slid from its back with a joyous, "Wheeeee!"

She wore running shoes that sparkled with lights as she walked. Pigtails and coveralls of pink over a gray T-shirt. Big eyes with a spark of Hell's flames perused him. Then a sweet girlish voice said, "Hi, I'm Lucinda. Lucifer is my grandpa. You're a reaper. You collect dead people. Can I play with your big knife?"

"Uh." He didn't actually manage a reply, but Helen did.

"No sharp things for children."

"But I like sharp things." Lucinda pouted as she turned to Helen, who sat on her heels, shocked and staring.

"They're dangerous," Helen reminded.

"You're an angel!" The little girl clapped her hands. "Like Daddy Auric."

"Your Father is an angel?" Helen asked.

Lucinda nodded. "I have two daddies. Daddy David is a kitty."

Given Helen's confused look, Julio jumped in to explain. "Lucinda's mother, Muriel, is the Dark Lord's daughter and has multiple mates." Then to the girl. "She will be pissed you are out here. It's dangerous."

The little girl blew a wet raspberry. "No, it's not. It's just a funny rock." She reached down and plucked the large egg-shaped stone that seemed to somehow shrink as she grabbed it.

"Put that down. It's dangerous," he barked.

Lucinda hugged it to her chest and said, "Pretty."

"Hand it over." He held out his hand.

"Mine." The girls clutched it tighter.

"It's not a toy. Give it to me." He reached for it, only to see the child stick it in her mouth.

Julio, having had many siblings who ate things they shouldn't, yelled, "Spit that out!"

With a glare of defiance inherited from her grand-Father, Lucinda swallowed. Burped. Then grinned. "Yummy, yummy in my tummy." By the time she finished the rhyme, the mist had evaporated, leaving a bleached, featureless land.

A second later, a rip appeared, and from it stepped Muriel, recognizable given all the news channels in Hell carried stories about her. She wore tight leather pants, a cropped top, and an angry expression.

She was quickly followed by Lucifer, then a fallen angel with the darkest look, a vampire who managed to appear even darker, a shapeshifter, a merman, and some woman with green hair. Muriel's harem.

They converged on Lucinda with Muriel exclaiming, "How did you get here, young lady?"

Lucinda beamed. "I was flying."

"This isn't the first ring where you're allowed to practice." Muriel wagged a finger.

"Oops." The child giggled.

"You could have gotten hurt!"

Julio felt like he should point out, "Your daughter swallowed the weird rock that appeared to be causing the mist."

Muriel glared at her kid. "What have I said about eating magical objects?"

Lucinda shrugged. "Tastes good."

"That's it, no dessert for a week," Muriel declared.

To which the child stamped her foot and said, "I want ice cream."

Did anyone else notice the crack zigzagging from the impact of her foot? Just him?

Lucifer sidled close. "Good job, Julio. I knew you could figure it out."

"No, you didn't." Even he caught that lie. Never mind the fact their escape was accidental. If Lucinda hadn't arrived, he had to wonder how long they would have wandered aimlessly before the egg ate Helen and, over time, maybe him, too.

Lucifer glanced around. "I don't suppose you found my missing eighth and ninth rings?"

"Does it look like I found part of your kingdom?" Julio snapped.

A barren gray landscape met their gaze. The only color in the distance being of the sliver of what was left of the eighth ring and the sight of falling ash. A glance overhead showed none drifting but the same even gray.

"I don't feel good." Lucinda held her tummy and moaned.

"I've got you, littlest lamb."

When the fuck had Bambi arrived? She held out a leather purse just as the child heaved and slammed it shut when done.

Julio eyed the purse. Was the egg inside? Did it matter? Everyone was safe.

Including his wife.

He swirled his cloak around her. "If we're done here, I'd like to find a place with a comfortable bed."

"And a toilet," Helen muttered.

Lucifer waved a hand. "Go."

"Where? Have you granted Helen asylum? Have you made her safe from the angels?"

"Don't worry. Everything will be just fine." For once, the devil's words didn't hold a lie.

Julio made the mistake of believing him.

22

THERE WAS relief in stepping into Julio's apartment on Earth. Helen might not have spent much time in it and yet the moment she saw the familiar setting, she felt herself relax.

"The door is fixed," she observed.

"Yup. But who cares when we can have a shower free of brimstone?"

"Just a shower?" She arched a brow.

It didn't take much coaxing to get her naked. Soon his soapy hands ran all over her body.

The moment he rinsed her clean, he was on his knees worshiping her, tonguing her sex, making her come against his mouth. Then making her cry out again as he pushed into her. The thickness of him stretching. Filling. Claiming.

Loving.

She celebrated each moment. Basked in happiness as Julio spent the next several days practically glued to her side and had her in every way imaginable. Bed. Shower. Counter. Couch. Window. Floor.

Even if she'd not been officially declared fallen, she sinned enough to be damned for eternity and she couldn't wait if it included Julio.

Eventually, though, they had to let the real world interfere. Julio had been handling his work via phone and computer, until it wasn't enough anymore.

"You have to go to work," she declared as he rubbed his face, having just hung up the phone.

"I'm not leaving you alone," he stated.

"Lucifer said things were fine."

"Since when do you believe anything the Dark Lord says?"

She pursed her lips. "Are you saying he lied?"

"I'm saying he has his own agenda that doesn't take into account other people."

"What should we do then?" Because, while new at this whole relationship thing, she knew they couldn't be together every second of every day. More than a few doctors on the internet said so when she did her research.

"Come with me to the office."

"To do what?"

"How about if we found you a job?"

"Then I could buy things." Her expression brightened, and after showing him how happy that made her, doing things with his man parts using her mouth that had him shouting, soon they were on their way to the Grim Dating offices.

Entering the building by his side, clutching his

hand, she couldn't help but notice the stares turning their way. Hearing the whispers.

"Why are they watching us?" she asked softly.

Julio grimaced. "Because I always swore I'd never get married."

"I'm sorry."

He glanced at her, startled. "Don't be. You should know by now I don't regret it."

She smiled. "It is nicer than I would have expected."

"Only nice?"

She leaned close enough for only him to hear. "There is nowhere I'd rather be than with you."

He apparently didn't care they had an audience as he swung her into his arms for a kiss. It lasted until someone yelled, "Get a room and don't forget to videotape it."

Julio growled, and she smiled. Grabbing his hand, she squeezed it before pulling him to the elevator. This time, she didn't have the same turmoil clutching her as they entered the office on the top floor. She'd learned so much since her first visit. Now she knew the truth. Knew what living could really be. Understood love. Definitely enjoyed the lust part.

She spent the next few hours inside the big office, the door open so she could see Julio at work while she took a course on the internet to learn how to be a nanny on Earth. The rules were different than she was used to. Apparently, holding a child and showing it affection helped it to grow. She could see the benefit.

Eventually, the latest client with a problem left and Julio came in with a sigh. "I swear, they don't read the fine print. We don't offer a guarantee. Sometimes a woman just has to accept a guy doesn't want to sleep with her on the first date."

"They don't like each other?"

"More like the client is determined to respect her and she just wants him to seduce her."

"Seduction is good." She leaned forward, bored with her studying and ready for more fun.

"Not yet. If I don't get us lunch first, my next appointment will arrive and then we'll both be hungry."

"I know what I'd rather eat."

Julio kissed her. "Hold that thought. I'll be right back with lunch, and if we're quick, we'll see how small that bathroom is."

Once Julio left, she paced, not realizing until that moment how much she relied on his presence. But this was good. She needed to do things on her own.

When the door opened, she expected to see him, only it wasn't Julio who walked in but Theodore.

And his grin was anything but angelic.

23

JULIO RETURNED to find Helen gone. The only sign she'd not left willingly was the feathers scattered on the floor.

"Lucifer!" he bellowed, not caring if he had any disrespect in his tone.

The Dark Lord appeared in a hazmat suit, holding a baby dressed in pink, exuding the most awful smell. "I'm kind of busy. Is it important?"

Ignoring the putrid stench, Julio snapped, "Helen was kidnapped!"

"No shit, Sherlock."

"By whom?"

"Who do you think?" The devil laid the baby on the desk and pulled forth some tongs to peel back her sleeper.

Julio pulled his shirt over his mouth and still it was as if he could taste it. "The angels got her? But I thought you said she was safe."

"Fake news. I said everything would be fine."

"How is it fine? They took her."

"Yup." The devil pulled free the shittiest diaper. It dripped as he yanked, the drops of liquid poop burning into the floor. Lucifer opened a rip into another dimension to drop it in.

"What are you going to do to get her back?" Julio asked, impatience burning, but knowing better than to blast the Dark Lord with his temper.

"Me? There's nothing I can do. She's in Heaven now."

Out of reach. Only Julio wouldn't give up. "So send the legion after her."

"And start a war? Over an angel? Don't be silly." The devil whipped out a sponge and swabbed the baby clean, drawing sweet giggles.

"It's not silly. She's my wife."

"Not anymore." The devil waved his hand in the air, and a sheet of paper tumbled from it. "My office just received the annulment."

"She loves me!" Julio's frustration boiled over.

"I doubt she'll remember that for long. Now that they've got their hands on Helen, my guess is they'll reprogram her. Teach her to follow the cult rules again."

Julio shook his head. "You're talking crazy. Helen knows Heaven is a scam. She doesn't want to be there."

"I hate to break it to you, but she will forget everything she experienced out here. Even you."

No. Julio refused to believe it. He could never forget the angel that showed him he still had a heart.

But as the days turned into weeks with no word

from her, he began to despair. Then he got angry, which, along with too many bottles of whiskey, led to his ill-advised plan.

HELEN STARED at the cherub in the crib. Sitting on his own, he stared right back. He had dark hair and a grin that, for some reason, reminded her of...

Julio smiling before he tossed an apple at her. She missed, and he showed her how to make it into a pie.

Pie was forbidden.

The memory slipped away, and she turned from the child, once more wondering why she'd been feeling out of sorts since her release from solitary.

Punished ninety days for leaving her room after curfew. Not that she remembered why she'd decided to go for a walk. She didn't even remember walking. One minute, she stood in the hall outside her door, full of fear at getting caught, and the next, she was on her knees, praying to her Father—*who is a liar*—in heaven.

Stray rebellious thoughts like that kept hitting her at random. Just like she kept seeing a face when she dreamed. Not just seeing the handsome face but kissing it. Indulging in fornication and waking achy between her legs. Missing someone she'd never met.

She must have a sickness. Never mind illness was rare. Something obviously ailed her because look at her stomach. Distended and hard to the touch.

Because I'm pregnant.

The shocking concept stole her breath. Angels didn't carry babies in their bodies. Animals did. Humans, too.

I'm half human.

The voice in her head wouldn't shut up, but Helen did her best to ignore it as she made her way from the nursery to the rooftop. Michelina already stood sentry, and Helen found it an effort to ignore her dislike of the other angel. What happened to feeling ambivalent?

"Surprised to see you back in the nursery," was Michelina snooty remark as they waited for a stork delivery.

"I did my penance and now serve our Father." Who hadn't been seen in a long time. Neither had his son. So who was running things?

"You should try exercising. You're getting fat," Michelina observed. Again, not something that happened usually. Most angels remained about the same size and weight, given their perfectly balanced meals and exercise.

Boring, disgusting gruel not fit for anyone.

"I think something is wrong with me." Helen cupped her belly.

Michelina tossed her head. "You'd better not be contagious."

Rather than reply, Helen pointed to the sky. "The stork is coming." And it appeared to struggle. Dipping and swerving, its wrapped bundle larger than usual and wiggling.

"What is wrong with that cherub?" Michelina exclaimed.

The baby continued to struggle and yell. The stork let out a caw of annoyance and dropped the baby. The oversized cherub landed in Helen's arms.

He stared at her. Then smiled. "Angel."

"Yes, I am." This was a first, an older child who could already talk.

"Helen." He said her name and patted her cheeks.

She had a flash of a place that wasn't Heaven. Not even close.

Of a woman—

Samantha

—-and a conversation about where cherubs came from.

As Helen gazed on the boy, she whispered, "Lector."

And remembered.

Everything.

Something must have warned Michelina, for she began to back away, her eyes wide. "Since you've got the cherub, I need to go."

"You!" Helen pointed, the child snug on her hip. "You tried to have me killed."

"I did not."

"I remember. You fornicated with Theodore." Helen grimaced, not because sex was gross but because she recalled all the ugly details of what happened.

Michelina lifted her chin. "You're obviously deranged. As if I'd break the rules."

At the obvious lie, Helen snorted. "Whatever. I know the truth now. And so should you. This is Theodore's son."

"You mean the Lord's child."

"Nope." Helen popped the P. "God doesn't make babies. Sex does."

"Blasphemy!" Michelina exclaimed.

"It's true. Male angels are sent to Earth to impregnate human females. The babies born with wings are then stolen and brought to Heaven by the storks." She gazed at Lector. "It's my fault you're here. I accidentally told Theodore about you."

"That is not his child. Liar. Liar." Michelina ran for the stairs, calling for the Archnanny, who would likely try and lock Helen up again for more memory washing.

Not happening. Never again.

Hitching Lector higher on her hip, Helen muttered, "What do you say I bring you back to your mommy?"

It felt good to take flight, soaring above the squat building and higher still over the walls enclosing the nursery. With all the secrets Heaven kept, no wonder they kept the nursery apart from other angels. Or was it just Helen who'd been blind to the truth for too long? Given how many times she was sent to solitary, she had to wonder if she'd stumbled across the truth before and had it taken from her.

As she soared, Lector clinging tight with chubby

fingers, she noticed a winged shape rising from the spreading city, arrowing toward her.

She refused to be locked away again. Not to mention, she had a stolen child to return. But where could she go? Who would help her stand against Heaven's army of angels?

Julio would. But he wasn't here.

A lone tower in the distance had her changing course, aiming for it and barely making it to the empty rooftop with no access inside. Oddly enough, the tower had no windows. No doors. It felt dull and solid. It also provided no succor.

Now what? From the corner of her eye, she caught a glint. A turn of her head showed the famed pearly gates, but before she could take flight, the soldiers of Heaven arrived, led by Theodore and flanked by four more warrior angels. Swords drawn. Expressions unkind. They landed on the tower.

She clutched Lector tight, and he whimpered against her. "Leave us alone."

"Hand over the child." Theodore clicked his fingers.

"He belongs with his mother."

"What are you talking about?" Theodore bluffed. "Our Father, who is fertile in Heaven, made this new brother."

Helen stamped her foot. "Stop the lies! Isn't it time everyone in Heaven knew the truth?"

"What truth? That you're one of the few dumb ones who believed everything she was told?" Theodore sneered.

"I was brainwashed."

"And you will be again," Theodore promised.

"You're evil."

"What are you going to do about it?"

"I'm going to pray." She crouched down and put her hand on the tower and whispered, "Our Father, who is imprisoned, if you're listening and have any love for me at all, help me escape. Me and this innocent child."

Then she rose suddenly and, with Lector clutched against her, ran for the edge. She knew she wouldn't make it without a miracle, but she had to try. To do nothing was to become a blind follower again.

She'd rather die.

Wings flapping, she aimed for the gates, her height dipping when she realized an ominous figure stood outside of them, dressed in a cloak that swirled around him like a mighty shadow. His stave planted on the white marble outside.

Julio didn't come alone. He had Kourtney in her deep blue robes by his side. They knocked at Heaven's door, the sound booming and drawing eyes.

It gave Helen the diversion she needed to pull ahead of Theodore, but when she would have flown over the gates, a force repelled her and she had no choice but to land. Ignobly she might add. Lector squawked.

"Sorry," she muttered.

Julio noticed her and bellowed, "Helen!"

"You came for me." The warmth inside her almost exploded.

He got right up against the gates and said, "I told you I wouldn't let you go."

She reached out and slid her hand through the bars so he could hold it. "I didn't want to leave."

"I know."

"Step away from the gate, reaper." Theodore landed and strode close, wearing a sneer.

"I've come for my wife."

"The marriage was annulled. She belongs to Heaven." Theodore's words crushed Helen.

"Actually, she doesn't." Kourtney held up a copy of the treaty between Heaven and Hell. "According to the eighteenth paragraph, subsection C, fallen angels are automatically the purview of Hell."

"She's not fallen," Theodore stated with his arms over his chest. "Our Father, who is on a break, hasn't cast her down."

"In this case, he's not needed to pass judgment because clause iii under subsection C states a female angel who gets pregnant shall be automatically considered fallen and cast out of Heaven."

"That's impossible." Theodore's gaze dropped to her belly.

A bunch of gazes did.

But not Julio's. He held her hand and mouthed, *I love you.*

Click. The gates opened without warning.

Julio tried to rush through but was stopped by the force field.

Helen took a step when she heard a voice, *Don't leave me, daughter. I will punish those who forsook you.*

But Helen couldn't forgive. *You lied to me.*

The tone of the voice changed. *You will obey. I am your God.*

Perhaps to others he was, but she'd decided to worship at a different altar. That of love.

She stepped through the gates and heard Theodore yelling at her back, "Kill the minion of Hell. She's kidnapping a cherub."

Theodore's soldiers remained still as he strode forward and reached for Helen, only to have Julio knock his hand away.

"Don't you fucking touch her."

"Or what? What will you do?" Theodore sneered some more as he drew his sword.

Helen tucked herself by Kourtney and set Lector on his feet as she watched.

"I'm not going to do a damned thing, actually. But I do wonder if maybe your god might have a thing or two to say." Julio stood bravely in front of the gates, and his cloak whipped as if caught in a storm.

"Our God is—"

"Angry," Lucifer said, as he appeared, wearing a somber dark suit. "And so am I. You locked my brother away."

"I didn't. His son did."

"And where is Charlie, my dear nephew?" Lucifer asked.

"He left and told us it was time we ruled ourselves." Michael was the one to provide the answer as he strode into view. "Given we are currently without a leader, I've been placed in charge of Heaven. Which means there will be some changes to how things are done."

Lucifer rubbed his hands. "Does this mean the treaty between Hell and Heaven is abolished?"

"I think it's past time we stopped playing this game." Michael held up a scroll that unrolled and kept unrolling. A silver flame ignited it.

As it turned into glittery ash, the devil smiled. "Here's to hoping you don't regret that later."

"We have no interest in Hell."

"And Earth?" Lucifer asked.

"Can govern itself," Michael declared.

"Well, you're definitely easier to deal with. Sounds fantastic. Good luck. Let's go, minions." Lucifer clapped his hands.

Julio pointed his stave in Theodore's direction. "What about him? I want a promise that he, and everyone else in Heaven, will leave Helen alone."

"And Lector!" Helen added.

Michael inclined his head. "Easy enough to arrange." The gates suddenly closed, leaving Theodore on the wrong side.

With a frown, Theodore moved to them and said, "Open up. Let me in."

The archangel now in charge offered a cold smile. "Only the unfallen can enter."

"I'm not fallen. God hasn't cast me down."

"Our Father isn't in charge anymore. I am. Your antics have the populace questioning my control. You will be an example to those who get too big for their wings. Enjoy Hell. You've earned it."

"No," Theodore screamed. "No, you can't do this."

"Apparently, he can, Theo old boy!" Lucifer beamed

as he rubbed his hands. "And wow, I'm impressed at your list of transgressions. How do you feel about spit shining boots for a few centuries?"

Theodore swung his sword at the devil and missed. By the time he pulled back to strike again, the devil snapped his fingers and the newly fallen angel was gone.

Kourtney tucked away her paperwork and said, "Just so you know, the annulment was invalid. It was filed after the child was conceived. You're still married."

Which was the thing Helen least cared about. She glanced at Julio then Lector. "We need to take him home to his mother."

"I'll handle it," Lucifer offered. "Hey, boy, ever hear about the time I ran with the wolves?" The pair disappeared, along with Kourtney, leaving Julio and Helen behind outside the closed pearly gates.

She'd never been more relieved to know they were shut to her forever.

She hugged Julio as she said, "Can we go home?"

"Sure. Where should we go?" Julio totally endorsed the idea of leaving. He still couldn't believe they'd manage to spring Helen. Especially since his plan had been more about drawing eyes on him while the real scheme happened in the background. A scheme that had failed to produce as expected.

Instead, he was saved by his pregnant wife.

Fuck him. She was carrying his child.

"I don't know," Helen mused loud. "It sounds strange to say, yet I didn't mind Hell. Although the food and television are better on Earth."

"My place, then?" he said to clarify as he began drawing the magic for the portal home.

She kissed his chin as she whispered, "My place is wherever you are."

So why not somewhere tropical? Julio adjusted his target location and stepped through with Helen.

The employees at the hotel in the Bahamas didn't bat an eye as they checked in, having arrived seemingly on foot with no luggage. His crimson credit card, registered with Hell's Only Bank, afforded them a villa on the ocean.

Helen's eyes widened with appreciation as he showed her true luxury. "This is so nice."

"Only the best for you, Curls." He closed the door and watched as she explored, suddenly not meeting his eyes.

"What's wrong? Are you upset about how things happened?" He'd worried she might not want to return, that her love for him would have been erased.

"No." She whirled and finally faced him. "I didn't want to leave. Theodore stole me, and then once they got me to Heaven, they tried to make me forget you."

He brushed a hand down her cheek. "I never stopped looking." The pearly gates tended to move around and, even if found, only opened for angels or acceptable souls.

Julio was neither. He'd spent many days stalking the entrance, trying to find a weakness.

She put her hand on his chest. "You came for me."

"Always, Curls. I'd die again for you. 'Cause I love you." He kissed her, and his world finally felt right again as she kissed him back.

The bed was wide enough for them to lie side by side, both their hands touching. Stripping clothes. Stroking.

He slid a finger into her and found her wet. Ready.

She sighed as he thrust into her. Then cried out as he kept grinding and fucking her until she damn well came hard and then pounded faster until she came again, milking him with the intensity of her orgasm.

He collapsed beside her but kept her tucked against his skin. Nuzzled her hair. And placed a hand on her belly. She lay hers atop.

"Does our child really grow in there?" she asked as if uncertain.

He couldn't speak, just nod, overwhelmed at the feel of the little person inside her.

"I love you," she said softly.

He made love to her again, gently, and yet it was powerful. Soul shaking.

As they lay together after, their bodies cooling, a shiver went through them, as if existence itself were shaken.

Helen gasped.

"What was that?" he asked.

"Our Father, who was angry in Heaven, has escaped."

EPILOGUE

RATHER THAN BRING Lector straight home, Lucifer made a pit stop because of a screaming baby, who, in turn, got her brother going.

Where was Gaia? She'd been reading them a story when he popped out to peek on Julio. Who, as it turned out, didn't need help at all because he'd impregnated an angel.

Good thing Lucifer had neutralized Elyon's sterility spell on the girl. He knew that clause in the contract about angels with a bun in the oven would eventually become useful.

"Waah!" Jujube's scream hit an epic note as he arrived with Lector perched on his shoulder, fingers dug in, a snarl on his face.

Junior quieted the moment Lucifer arrived and pretended he'd not been crying at all. He knew how his Father felt about appearing weak.

As for Jujube, she was a drama llama.

"What's wrong, princess?" he cooed.

As Jujube opened her mouth to lament, Lector barked, "Baby, stop crying."

The demand halted Jujube mid yodel. She blinked wet lashes as she took in Lector. Her gaze narrowed before she hiccupped, "Mine."

Lector snorted as he leapt off Lucifer's shoulder and fluttered to the floor by the crib. "I'm not a baby toy."

Jujube pouted. "Da gimme."

"No." Lector shook his head and checked out the room. His presence fascinated both Junior and Jujube.

Junior grabbed the bars of his crib and climbed. The lid Lucifer just had installed was no match for his Houdini skills. Apparently, Junior had been paying attention in class with the damned magician. Soon Junior toddled after Lector, pointing out toys of interest, while Jujube got upset at being stuck in her crib.

She uttered a plaintive sound that drew attention. Junior sneered, not at all taken in by his sister, who didn't play nice.

But Lector returned to her crib and asked, "You want to play, too?"

Jujube nodded.

"Okay." Lector grabbed the bars and climbed to the top. There was no lid yet. Not much point given Jujube could blast it to splinters if she wanted.

Lector hopped into the crib, and Jujube reached for him. "Mine."

The boy shook his finger. "No. Play."

Jujube smiled. "My boy."

Having been a matchmaker for a while, Lucifer recognized that tone. He finally interfered and pulled

Lector out of his daughter's reach. "Don't you go claiming him yet, princess. I've got bigger plans for you. But he will make a good bodyguard."

It was as if his daughter understood because she nodded, and Lector, squirming in Lucifer's grip, quieted.

"Good. Because you'll need each other if the future goes the way I plan."

"Daddy." Junior's warning tone had them all quieting. Listening. Feeling the ominous presence pressing against the wards around the nursery. Testing them.

For a moment, the smell of roses and decay filled the room.

No one breathed, not even the devil.

The entity left, but it would return. Hopefully by then Jujube would be able to defend herself, and today would start Lector's path as one of her defenders.

And not a moment too soon as a shiver went through Hell. A sudden wave of force that had Lucifer's eyes widening.

Elyon has escaped! And an angry God was a vengeful one. The world was about to see why people used to worship Lucifer's brother eons ago. And if they refused to bow? Flooding the world was the least of their worries. This time around, Elyon had the power to do worse.

While Lucifer had been collecting the souls of the wicked, his brother had been storing those of the unborn. Those killed before they could ever sin.

It turned out that was the more lucrative way of

accumulating souls. If you wanted spirits with no personality.

Personally, Lucifer liked humans with all their many flaws. Loved their minds, their creations, and fed on their emotions. He especially enjoyed his own progeny, who took after him in many ways.

Blart.

"Ew. Baby farted!" Lector declared.

To which Lucifer said, "Good girl."

Today she passed harmless gas. Starting tomorrow, he'd teach her how to poison armies because war was coming.

AND SO IS A WEDDING BECAUSE BAMBI APPEARS TO BE ENGAGED, HER RING SET with the strange stone Lucinda tried to swallow. But has she truly found love, or is her fiancé using her to get to the devil? Stay tuned for news on Lucifer's Other Daughter ~ *Bambi's autobiography.*

For more stories please see http://www.EveLanglais.com

Newsletter: http://evelanglais.com/newrelease

9 781773 842103